LIBERATION

THE LAZARUS ALLIANCE, BOOK 5

BLAZE WARD

Liberation
The Lazarus Alliance: Book Five
Blaze Ward
Copyright © 2021 Blaze Ward
All rights reserved
Published by Knotted Road Press
www.KnottedRoadPress.com

ISBN: 978-1-64470-203-1

Cover art:

ID 82691116 © Luca Oleastri | Dreamstime.com

Cover and interior design copyright © 2021 Knotted Road Press

Reviews
It's true. Reviews help. Even a short one, such as, "Loved it!" So please consider reviewing this book (and all of the ones you've read) on your favorite retailer site.

Never miss a release!
If you'd like to be notified of new releases, sign up for my newsletter.

http://www.blazeward.com/newsletter/

Buy More!
Did you know that you can buy directly from my website?

https://www.blazeward.com/shop/

Phoenix

Princess Rualoh

ONE

LAZARUS

LAZARUS SAT in his command chair on the bridge of the Light Starcruiser *Ajax*, his first true love, and watched the screens empty. Once, he would have said only love, but he was pretty sure he'd be lying at this point, thinking about what he and Grace were in the process of carving out in the middle of so many wars.

The weirdest part had been going to Addison for advice, as the man had only recently allowed himself to admit to himself or Eha his feelings, and the two of them were now as bonded as they could be without actually filing the correct legal paperwork someplace like Gowook.

But then, how do you do something like that when you are in open rebellion against that same government?

Addison had simply told Lazarus to get over himself and steal every moment he could while off duty, so Lazarus had. Grace had no interest in joining the navy and coming under military discipline, but she turned her head and smiled at him now as if she had been listening to his thoughts, sitting quietly off to one side of the bridge. Out of the way, but close if needed.

That rather described her in more ways than one.

Dark skin and curly ringlets from her pure West African ancestry, unlike folks whose ancestors might have crossed *América do Norte* before heading into space and eventually arriving at a place like Yisan.

Grace wasn't from that pirate world. Lazarus hadn't pressed on learning too much of her life story, once he was sure that she had been trained as a geisha in the fullest sense of the word. And an assassin. It was enough to know that they might manage something, assuming he didn't get himself killed in one of the stupid wars he was fighting.

"Addison is away," Wybert of Capantzina, Lt. Commander and Fusilier, announced from his station. He was handling *Ajax*'s sensors since he had nothing to shoot at and the ship was even more short-handed with several folks over on the little patrol cutter.

Captain Carlos Nguema, aboard the Patrol Cruiser *Dutra*, had offered some crew members, but he had also been short-handed, as he had had to send officers home with the three captured Westphalian ships. Everyone was stretched thin, but they would manage.

Lazarus nodded to himself. *Ajax* was alone, now that the captured Westphalian ships were heading to Yisan for internment and the refugee colony ships were all headed to Vilga's Stand with Rio Alliance High Councilor Erlyn Teixeira aboard as an escort.

The ship formerly named *Astral Jewel* hadn't even emitted the usual redshift that Lazarus always expected when a ship jumped. The vessel had been captured from the Innruld, and used trans-space drives. Slower than *Ajax* to get anywhere, except where Lazarus had to land and turn to hop around things, while Addison could just sail around corners. That had been helpful in the Phraettis Nebula, but they were in deep space now.

Lazarus smiled one last time at Grace and turned the other direction to the man standing on his right.

"Admiral," Lazarus said, drawing the man's eyes back from the big screen at the front of the bridge. "Welcome to Innruld Space."

Rodrigo da Silva had gone gray at a very young age, and routinely dyed his hair black, but that was about his only affectation. Lazarus had served under the man in the past, and known him as a senior officer for nearly a decade. Solid. And absolutely the right man for the job here, to sail into the unknown and possibly start a war.

His reddish-brown skin split the difference between Lazarus's pale freckles and Grace's rich brown, but da Silva's ancestors had been Brazilian on the homeworld, long before they emigrated to the stars and helped found the Rio Alliance to resist the specists of Westphalia.

The man smiled at him now, but it was almost more of a grimace than anything. That was the weight of history riding on his shoulders. Lazarus had discovered Innruld Space for the Rio Alliance, but da Silva would go down as the first true representative of the Alliance to visit. And the man who would command the war of liberation that Lazarus hoped to finally initiate.

"I see you, and my mind keeps wanting to call you *Pancho*," da Silva said, his face finally moving closer and closer to a smile. "I suppose, given all the symbology present, that might make me Saul of Tarsus, wouldn't it? I didn't really believe you, even when I finally met Eha and Aileen face to face, and now, here I am, about to support you in this craziness. Does that make sense?"

Lazarus gestured to the screen, showing clear space finally, after the tight confines of the Phraettis Nebula for so long.

"It does, if you look at this as one of the roads to Damascus, Admiral," Lazarus said.

"No, call me Rod," he said. "This is not an officially sanctioned voyage of exploration into Innruld Space. Well, it is, but that was just to sail as far as Dormell or Zhoonarrim and open negotiations with them. I don't see that happening. Time is tight and risks are too great."

"So what would you call it, Rod who might be Piotr?" Lazarus grinned at the man.

"Oh this is pure piracy, youngster," Rod grinned back. "Naval guerrilla warfare 101. We just happen to be far stronger than the ships sneaking around, but it doesn't change anything. We still have to prevent Innruld and Westphalia from meeting each other. The Innruld won't understand how little chance they have, and Westphalia won't stop until they conquer or annihilate everything in their path."

"They will not," Lazarus said in a voice so sharp and hard that all the heads in the room came around to stare at him. He smiled at them. "But Westphalia will still have to go through us first."

TWO

EHA

LOOKING around the conference room at the key players, Eha wasn't sure how she had come to be in supreme command of this rag-tag squadron, except that nobody else was in a position to do it. Her mother knew all the rebels they were escorting. Councilor Teixeira knew her and Captain Nguema, the Gnashiiley in charge of the ship she was aboard.

But hadn't she taken upon herself the title Ambassador to the Humans? Or at least to the Rio Alliance? She hadn't met Westphalia yet, at least not directly. The late and unmissed Strav Ardna might have been Westphalian. Or just an asshole. Either way, the galaxy was a better place with him dead.

Eha gasped inside at herself. When had she gotten so callous about shedding blood? Except that nobody could rate Ardna as an innocent. He had fired the first shots in their little war. And the second and third. His mistake had been in not understanding that her friends would fire the last ones.

And she had always known that the Innruld would not cede power willingly. Hadn't she spent the better part of a decade overseeing the smuggling of a certain chemical that only affected the Innruld? Induced lethargic euphoria to the point that users just wanted to lay around all day being mellow?

Addison had called them termites in the foundation, slowly gnawing away until the structure fell in on itself.

And now the storm had finally arrived.

She turned to Captain Nguema and studied the man. Gnashiiley. Shorter than a Human by a head and covered over with fur and stripes. In Innruld Space, they tended to be more red, while in Rio they were more gray-brown. Long, slender face with a snout and black nose that Humans called kitsune after a mythical creature.

He sat across from her at the small table, with Alla on her left and Erlyn on her right.

The keys to liberation were here at this table.

"Is there anything else we need to cover today?" Eha asked, bringing the meeting back on track after it had wandered.

"We have arrived at the third checkpoint," Nguema replied. "At this point, we are waiting for the squadron to follow us through trans-space, but they are much slower, being commercial vehicles at the low end of reliability."

"Would it be better to put some of your spare engineers aboard those ships to help with repairs?" Teixeira asked, a beat before Eha could.

But they had spent a lot of time across a negotiating table before this, so Eha knew how the woman thought.

Nguema, for his part, shrugged.

"Completely alien technology, ladies," he said. "Granted, mechanical engineering is universal, but they'd still be lost."

"Perhaps," Alla spoke up now, Eha's mother leaning forward like a predator about to strike. "But none of those vessels are crewed by military folks. I have asked some of your permanent crew members what it has meant that you brought extra engineers from Brasilia, and the consensus has been entirely positive, if only for having extra hands to do things. We would move faster if all ten of those ships were less prone to breaking down. That means you get to return to Innruld Space that much faster."

Everyone smiled at that. There wasn't much greater of a bribe you could use to lever the man, since he was no longer participating in the greatest adventure of all time, the one they had left behind with Addison and Lazarus.

"I'm not sure I'll be allowed," Nguema said after a momentary grimace. "Anything might have happened while we were gone, and the fleet might have managed to send reinforcements, which would probably include an admiral who could give me orders."

"No, he could not," Teixeira said bluntly. "This is still a diplomatic mission, which means you answer to me until I or the High Council say otherwise, Captain. You continue doing the right thing by everyone and I'll run interference."

"What about the war?" Eha turned to the Human Councilor now. "You cannot be in two places at once, Erlyn. We are about to deliver an entire, new colony of aliens to the Rio Alliance's doorstep, and someone will need to interface with the High Council. And Addison and Lazarus will need you in Innruld Space to work with the Species Underground, of which this colony is just the tip of a much larger iceberg."

Erlyn Teixeira turned to her with a smile that had Eha's scales flaring up, not just around her eyes but halfway down to her tail.

"I have had many thoughts on that topic, Eha," she said slowly. "One in particular sounded quite interesting."

"Oh?" Eha asked, already not liking it, even as much as she liked and respected this woman.

"So the Rio Alliance currently represents four species,"

Erlyn continued. "Human, Gnashiiley, Moah, and Atomarsk. Humans are the largest group by far, but the High Council itself has always included at least one representative of the four species, regardless of the demographics."

She paused, studying Eha's eyes. Alla gasped and distracted Eha.

"What?" Eha asked her mother, but Teixeira spoke instead.

"A new colony at Vilga's Stand represents eleven new species, but the refugees are more than fifty percent Churquen," Erlyn smiled. "I think that Alla would make a good planetary governor for now, while the Rio Alliance figures out what to do with the arcane legalisms of people technically illegally settling on a closed colony. I presume that the investors will just be reimbursed for whatever fractional loss they sustain, and perhaps a few other things. They may not even face a loss, as the remainder of those two worlds might become far more valuable real estate when all is said and done."

"And me?" Eha asked.

"I think you should continue to be the first Ambassador to the High Council, as you were before, but with an eye towards possibly becoming the first Churquen High Councilor, Eha," Teixeira concluded.

Eha's eyes got so big they were painful. The light was so bright she was blinded, so she concentrated on closing her eyeslits back down.

"Oh," she managed after a couple of seconds.

Was that even possible? What would it mean to her and Addison, and her unborn child, who might be the first Churquen born in a Rio world?

Alla and Captain Nguema smiled, so they seemed to support it, but Eha had one misgiving.

"What about Addison?" she asked. "If all that happens, I won't be able to see him until he returns to Rio space."

"I understand," Erlyn commiserated. "But this is going to be so much bigger than the two of you, Eha. This will set the course for species relations for the next century. We need to do it right."

Eha could see that. Could see the brilliance of such a maneuver in Teixeira's hands. The colony would be in good hands with her mother. Teixeira would return to Innruld Space.

And Eha Dunham might become a High Councilor.

How had they all gotten here?

THREE

OLUCHI

OLUCHI SURVEYED the remains of dinner and belched happily. It wasn't that he'd been served bad food in the past, but with Fernanda Flores arriving from Yisan as something of a legal Ambassador, she'd also brought her personal chef. And *that* woman was amazing.

Anya reached over and refilled his glass from the carafe before filling hers and leaning back. Oluchi beamed at the two women and wondered just how bad it must have been in a previous life that he got this today.

"So, Mr. Ambassador to the Species Underground," Fernanda said over a glass of what had turned out to be a lovely red she'd brought with her from one of her estates. "What's next on your agenda?"

"How serious is Eduardo Martìnez about allowing Yisan to possibly become closer trading partners with the Rio Alliance?" Oluchi fired back. "Or even actually applying for membership and presumably bringing thirty to fifty more worlds with you?"

"What's his favorite phrase?" Fernanda laughed. "*Money talks and bullshit sits on the curb grumbling*? Even with the worlds of Innruld Space being so distant and so primitive, that just means that folks with old factories can squeeze new life out of them, or dig up things out of patent or in the collective commons and make a quick killing. There are a lot of people who will have industrial needs, if nothing else."

"An enterprising someone might just dismantle an old factory here and ship everything there," Oluchi observed.

But then, he'd spent a lot of time as a boytoy among Fernanda's crowd, being passed around among the various ladies or playing poker with Eduardo's circle. You learned a lot, just listening.

"Ah, but nobody has coordinates right now," Anya spoke up with a sarcastic gleam in her eyes. "Our poor Ambassador might just be selling a pig in a poke."

Oluchi made a face at her, but she just smiled.

"What will you do, if they don't come back for you?" Fernanda turned serious.

Both women turned to face him now, but Oluchi just sipped at the wine and thought happy thoughts, glad that he didn't also have to face Erlyn Teixeira right now. Three more dangerous, beautiful Human women he could not imagine. Eha and Aileen didn't count on this dangerous score because they weren't Human.

"I'm sure I could convince someone to fund me a ship," Oluchi belched again. "But I doubt that it will come to that."

"Why not?" they both managed in perfect tandem.

"Lazarus didn't come back from Vilga's Stand," Oluchi said. "Then the fleet sent Addison in another vessel. Someone will find their way over. At that point, the greater risk will be a flood of refugees hoping that the Rio Alliance will take them in and succor them against the Innruld. That's why I have been working my ass off on the treaty side of things, so that when Eha gets back, she or whoever she sends can sign it and we're on firmer legal ground."

Anya stirred and fixed him with a more sober look. Oluchi felt *serious* creep up on him, but he refused to allow it to ruin his evening. He just stared at her, owl-like. Fernanda picked up the change and got quiet as well.

Staring, but he wasn't about to speak first. She'd started it.

Anya leaned forward now, elbows on either side of her empty dessert plate. A burp snuck out and she turned red for a moment.

"Yisan," she said quietly.

Oluchi nodded.

"They used to be kind of the ends of known space," Anya continued.

Oluchi nodded some more, still unsure where she was going. He sipped the red and listened.

"But Lazarus was coming from Innruld Space, and they were close enough to his line of flight to make a detour," she pressed on, possibly gaining steam now, except that she ran out of words.

And blushed again.

"Talk to me," Oluchi implored her, aware that the conversation had stopped being light.

At one point, he'd asked her about what they did with old spies, and if she might be interested in a life after espionage with him in it. The look in her eyes was the same it had been when he'd quoted Gibran to her.

"There is a lot of money being tossed around, even in the theoreticals," Anya finally said, but now she was looking right at Fernanda, so Ms. Flores nodded.

"Until you've done deals with that many commas in the numbers, they seem like fairy tales," Fernanda replied. "Eduardo asked me to come because he could see where Oluchi here might be stepping up to agreements equal to

Planetary Domestic Product numbers, just for the increase in trade we might see."

"Oluchi has infected me," Anya said.

He wanted to make a joke about seeing her doctor, but she'd turned deadly serious now.

Fernanda just nodded.

"I want at least a small piece of that," Anya said. "Oluchi thinks that he'll get filthy, stinking rich, just on percentages, but he still won't be anywhere near the scale where you or Eduardo or some of the others are, will he?"

"No," Fernanda replied soberly. "Eduardo is the only one who might make the top hundred for net worth on Brasilia, but once you leave this cosmopolitan planet, he's going to be in the top dozen, almost anywhere else you want to go in Human Space."

"Will he send out ships exploring while you are here?" Oluchi turned to Fernanda now. Not a hard look, but more than merely curious.

"We discussed it," Fernanda replied honestly. "But quickly realized that we'd lose control of the situation if we did, and potentially burn bridges with Rio, at the time when they might be in a position to win the war with Westphalia and establish a new *Pax Galactica*. Lazarus deeply impressed a number of people. His offhand comment about burning our planet to the ground got through."

Oluchi turned back to Anya now, studying her.

"Where are you going with this?" he asked her gently.

"Should the two of you head to Yisan at some point?" she asked. "Maybe start building new orbital platforms and shipping warehouses for the trade that we all know is going to start rolling in shortly?"

"Would you come with me if I did?" he asked her, circling back to that topic that they had danced around, but never really settled.

"Would you have me?" Anya asked.

"I'm not sure I could go without you," Oluchi said simply.

She smiled all the way to the bottom of her soul and turned to Fernanda.

"Can I borrow a hundred million or so to get things rolling?"

Fernanda grinned.

"Let's discuss some sweat equity, first," she countered.

Oluchi gestured to the palace around them that had been his home for months and hers for a few weeks now. The deals he had already done, and the various fires he had in the pot, just waiting for everything to come together.

"Top this," he declared.

FOUR

ADDISON

ADDISON DIDN'T ACTIVELY DISLIKE Eha's *Astral Jewel*, the security ship that Lazarus and Eha had stolen from the Innruld. Looking around the bridge, the Humans had done an admirable job of rebuilding and fixing everything, to the point that it was far more dangerous than any other vessel in this weight category.

It just wasn't *Shiva Zephyr Glaive*. Granted, nothing leaked or shorted out nearly as badly as his old cargo transport, but it still wasn't home. And he would be in command of this beast until Rodrigo da Silva got enough reinforcements or trained crews that Addison could finally go back to what he wanted in life.

Except thaiswouldn't happen at that point, either. Being director on a broken-down cargo tramp wasn't going to be socially acceptable if he was permanently joined with the Churquen or Species Underground Ambassador to the Rio Alliance. She'd probably make him buy a nicer ship, at the very least, just so the old one could be retired into a museum of inter-species communications or something.

That old Atomarsk miner had made a killing, selling his

ship to the Humans for exactly that purpose, but Addison hadn't had a chance to visit the museum when he was on Brasilia. Too busy doing other things.

That busyness wasn't going to change, anytime soon. And he really only had half his crew with him, with Kuei, Wybert, and Aileen behind him aboard *Ajax*. Also, he wasn't hauling cargo so much as revolution. In that, they had renamed the ship and reworked the engine transmitters so that it would call itself *Star of Kilri* when pinged.

None of the stars deep in the Phraettis Nebula had names, because supposedly nobody had been that far to explore them. But the system where he had first rescued Lazarus had taken on a greater meaning now. Doubly so when they'd returned and found *Ajax*. Trebly when they had fought the first battle between the three sides here, even if it had been Lazarus in command.

But Kuei had decided to call that system *Kilri* on her maps, part of Akeley's Passage that would eventually connect the two sides of the galaxy.

So Addison was flying the *Star of Kilri*. Well, Cormac was. They were headed for another one of those corner spars of Innruld Space that stuck out like the tentacles of a drunk squid.

Oton Mari. Another dead end, but one that focused on serving regional miners more than trade. Or maybe preying on them, since it was a company town and you either had to pay their rates for things or fly deeper into Innruld Space, balancing time and effort against cost.

Addison had always had a low-grade burning hatred of the Innruld, but until very recently, there had never been alternatives. He had once dedicated his existence to bringing the Innruld down, just because of what they did to all the other species at places like Oton Mari.

And now he could.

Addison shivered to the tip of his tail, wrapped around the cone they had installed for him as director/owner of this new-old ship.

"*Everything within tolerable limits, old friend?*" Cormac asked, rotating a camera aft.

It was weird, seeing him still in the tan of the Rio Alliance Navy with lieutenant's pips, when everyone else had reverted to civilian attire, but only a Human would look at that color as anything other than a new paint job.

"You and I have been working towards this for a long time, Cormac," Addison replied.

Cormac had been with him the longest of all the current crew, nearly two decades. Longer than he had known Eha or the Species Underground.

"*Indeed,*" Cormac agreed. "*I occasionally wonder if we are doing the right thing, but Lazarus has infected me with a revolutionary fervor possibly unique among my kind.*"

Addison nodded.

"And I as well, Cormac," Addison agreed. "You and I have moved beyond what the Humans call guerrilla warfare and are actively working to destroy the Innruld. It liberates me as much as it frightens me."

"*What will Eha Dunham do, when she is in a position to decide what happens to the surviving Innruld?*" Cormac asked.

Addison shuddered again. That was a pointedly cogent question.

Addison was certain that his rage at the system would spill over into a xenocidal drive to end the Innruld entirely, but she had always been more the diplomat on that topic.

Except that she wasn't here.

Eha Dunham would not be present at that key moment, when two killers named Addison Wolcott and Lazarus of Bethany held the fate of the Innruld in their hands.

And Addison finally saw himself as a killer, even if

Wybert was the one who pushed the buttons. The Fusilier had been following orders from Addison Wolcott, the greatest alien killer of Humans to date.

"Cormac, I need you to do me a favor," Addison replied after a long beat to consider.

"*Yes?*"

"Ask me that exact question when it comes time to decide," Addison said.

"*Addison?*"

"She will not be here to speak for herself, most likely, Cormac," he said. "So we need to remember that there are alternatives to killing all of them and forcing the Creator of All to reconcile their souls for us."

"*Will it come to that?*" Cormac asked in a remarkably organic voice. But then, he had over a century of uptime at this point.

"The Innruld have not yet met *Ajax*, old friend," Addison pointed out. "Look what Lazarus did, alone in a bar against six Innruld. Their arrogance will be an immovable object about to meet the irresistible force of the Rio Alliance, and I do not believe that they are immovable anymore."

"*A single leaf in the face of the hurricane,*" Cormac suggested.

"Yes," Addison agreed. "And you and I are about to become the heralds of destruction."

FIVE

LAZARUS

WHEN HE HAD DESIGNED *AJAX*, Lazarus had been working with the specific size and shape of Kirov's Lance, so the vessel was long and slender like a goose. But that had also meant that he had a tremendous amount of volume he could fill, just by adding on bits and pieces here and there. With those three big wings, one hundred and twenty degrees apart, he even got a pretty good amount of optical parallax for passive sensors and telescopes. Useful for long range sniping too, but as a result, he could sit off at a tremendous distance from someplace and watch someone quietly.

The risk of a blueshift lighting up the night sky had meant that *Ajax* needed to come out at Oton Mari way out from the station and planet, and then sail down closer. He wasn't going to encounter anybody because Innruld ships would emerge from trans-space almost on top of the station. And he flew much faster than the *Star of Kilri*, so they had come here directly and waited.

Lazarus was on the bridge with both Kuei and Wybert, mostly killing time as they let the navigational systems read the entire solar system passively while they waited for Addison to catch up.

Addison had mentioned that the station served the region as a mining services hub. The planet below produced food, but that was about it, as all industrial machinery came from deeper in. Innruld-owned factories. Just another trap for the miners.

They had scanned nearly a hundred vessels coming and going. Most of them were small, just a box with engines and a tiny apartment attached, rather than a big industrial vessel. Hardy individuals who went out to try and find an asteroid somewhere that contained valuables. Maybe the heart of a gas giant that had been blasted into deep space by a supernova and could be recovered.

Anything to make a little money and maybe prosper under Innruld rule.

The station itself was different than the ones Lazarus had seen at Dormell or Zhoonarrim. Instead of the traditional castle-shape, where you had to fly inside and land, this was a large conglomeration of boxes with docks attached. Made sense, if you had to deal with dozens of miners at any given moment, coming and going on a random schedule.

Might make smuggling easier, as well, but Addison had mentioned that there were far more security officers here than most places. Again, dealing with potentially rowdy miners.

The sorts of men and women who might make excellent revolutionaries.

"Hey, that's interesting," Wybert spoke up.

He'd been studying everything through the lens of destroying it with the big cannon, but that was Wybert. He had finally turned into the sort of Ilount who would be allowed to mate with a queen one of these days.

"Show me," Lazarus called, bringing up his screens and

turning off maintenance records from Aileen that he had been reviewing.

"A new Security Pyramid just came out of trans-space." Wybert brought up the big main screen and highlighted a brighter light than most of the rest.

Lazarus watched him dial in the zoom.

They were ziggurats, like the Innruld built on the surface of their planets as well. Broad squares with back-sloping walls, stepping back regularly until they came up to a penthouse where the Director and important people resided. Pyramids did not move fast, but were at least as heavily armed as a patrol cruiser like *Dutra*. And probably as tough as a Heavy Starcruiser, but that was a factor of mass more than anything. A vessel that would cover a square mile of ground if it ever landed had to be tough, just to fly.

Kirov's Lance would still hit it like a harpoon, regardless of how big that silly whale was.

"Should there be a Pyramid around here?" Lazarus asked.

He'd been a spacer among these folks for only a matter of months, such that much was still opaque.

"Well, maybe," Wybert replied. He turned to look at his partner expectantly with a drum of his back two feet on the pad she had taped to the deck. "Kuei?"

"They travel around a lot," she took up the narrative now, sitting a little straighter. "Mostly to cow various systems that have been feeling feisty, because there's nothing in Innruld Space that can stand up to them. At least not until we got here. Plus, they carry a lot of troops so they can board any number of vessels and inspect them. Good way to crack the whip on folks."

"So they might be here because Oton Mari is a haven for troublemakers?" Lazarus asked expectantly.

"Yup," she replied, turning to smile at him over her inner shoulder. "But that's why we're here, right?"

"It is," Lazarus smiled back.

He thought about it for a few moments and keyed a line aft.

"Security, Lam here," Lucas replied.

Lucas Lam was a Rio Alliance Lieutenant who had been assigned to Eha as a bodyguard back when she first arrived at Brasilia, and had been with the team since then. Lazarus had originally intended to leave him in charge of station security when he'd captured the Westphalian base at Vilga's Stand, but Lucas and Xiuying had swapped billets, and Lucas had gone on to Innruld Space.

"Channel four has optics on an Innruld Security Pyramid that has just arrived in-system," Lazarus told the man. "I realize that you don't have a full battalion of troops with you, but your task is to study the design and anything else we can find out, in case we end up fighting this one."

"Wouldn't you blowtorch him into pieces if it came to battle, sir?" Lucas asked.

"Maybe," Lazarus agreed. "But even those pieces would still be relatively intact. They would just be carved off like turkey meat. Someone would need to board and round up survivors. Possibly fight a pitched battle in the corridors, with or without gravity. Your job is to plan for how we do that."

"On it, sir," Lucas replied.

Lazarus cut the line and studied the beast. *Ajax* was a long, graceful bird in flight. That pyramid was an ugly hunk of architecture. Brutalism in steel, designed to impress people who had to bow the knee.

Lazarus was looking forward to having a conversation with those folks at some point.

SIX

EDUARDO

EDUARDO MARTÌNEZ SAT on the enclosed back patio of his mansion and enjoyed his breakfast. He was dressed for a casual day today, instead of the formal suits he normally wore in public. Slacks and a gray cable knit sweater against the fall chill. Easy.

A widower now for eleven years, with his children all grown and off running various facets of the company they would eventually own, he liked to keep things quiet on the home front.

Not for him the sorts of grand adventures he had undertaken sixty years ago. The risks. Occasionally, he missed the excitement, but these days he was having fun just disrupting all of Yisan.

Once a sleepy pirate haven where a young man with a penchant for luck, risks, and finance might make a name for himself, Eduardo's life's work had turned it into a place. Certainly, there were still pirates around, but most of them were privateers these days, working under contract and subject to rules.

Just not Westphalian or Rio Alliance rules for the most part.

And then Eha Dunham and Aileen Enjehn had arrived. Everyone else had spent a week or more mourning the sudden and *accidental* death of Strav Ardna, but Eduardo had pivoted instantly and started planting the seeds of the future.

An alien one, with Yisan as an off-ramp to a brand new superhighway that folks were just starting to think about, even as he was pouring concrete. Eduardo suspected that the aliens were near or maybe even in the Phraettis Nebula, but had ordered every one of his ships deeper into Human Space, rather than let anyone go looking.

He and Fernanda had concluded that they would get the coordinates they needed soon enough, and that it would be better to deal with Rio at that point.

Eduardo sipped at his coffee as Janice removed his plates with a smile. She'd been with the household for twenty years now, and was going to retire soon to a place on the ocean that she and her husband had been patiently building with wages and occasional bonuses.

Collin appeared as she entered the main building, his normally serious face displaying honest emotion today. Confusion, of all things.

Eduardo wasn't sure if that was a sign of the apocalypse or not, considering Collin was his Assistant Business Manager, a rather pedestrian title for one of the most important and powerful operatives in his entire organization.

Collin was tall, but much skinnier than Eduardo. Dressed like a banker in sober grays, but that was Collin. He'd probably already been up for two hours tracking the various news while the rest of the city slept. Mid-thirties. Well-educated. Smart. Canny, which was what Eduardo valued in the young man. Able to think on his feet and react quickly when everything went sideways. As appeared to have happened now.

Collin approached diffidently, as if unsure what words to use.

"Sit," Eduardo ordered him. "Have some coffee while you process."

Better to let the man get it straight in his own head. This was more than just a run on one of the banks Eduardo owned. It might actually be serious.

They drank coffee for a few minutes until Collin's color turned better. He sat his cup down silently and took a breath.

"We have been hailed from orbital space, Eduardo," he said simply. "The person calling identifies herself as a Rio Alliance Naval officer, asking specifically for you."

"Indeed?" Eduardo asked.

He'd been expecting something like this. Eha and Aileen had already greatly disrupted Brasilia. Oluchi Pryce, of all people, had kept the ball rolling nicely, claiming to be an agent of Eduardo and others on Yisan, there to negotiate trade and treaties with the aliens. How better to keep those Rio politicians honest?

Eventually, things had gotten so intense and complicated that Fernanda Flores had volunteered to go check up on her former boy-toy and see how the lad was doing.

They must have had fun if the Rio Alliance Navy was calling on him now.

"It gets more complicated, Eduardo," Collin said, gritting his teeth as he spoke. "The woman in charge is flying aboard a trio of Westphalian GunWall ships."

Eduardo was certain that he would have spilled his coffee if the cup wasn't empty. He turned to Collin and studied the man's face, certain that he had misheard.

"Yes," Collin said. "They claim to be vessels captured by Lazarus in alien space and transported here under ransom-flag. The woman says that she is authorized to sell the vessels to you or some other Yisan authority if you weren't available, with some portion of the funds dedicated to transporting five crews of Westphalian sailors back to Earth or the closest naval port."

Eduardo took a deep breath. Considered all the possible outcomes that he had written down in his safe to prepare for this day.

None of them were anywhere near this big. This symbolic.

This *disruptingly* dangerous.

The entire galaxy had just changed in the last ten seconds.

"Contact Beauregard and cancel or reschedule everything on my calendar for the next ninety-six hours," Eduardo decided, instantly assuming that anything he had planned was already wrong. "Arrange passage to the orbital platform for me and a staff including you. Bring some bankers and someone who can do naval assays, so we can buy those ships outright if we want to. Charter enough cruise ships to handle all the Westphalian crews in something pleasant when you get a count and put the Rio Alliance crew up in a penthouse somewhere, away from anyone outside our organization who might want to meddle, especially if she asked for me first. Pack for at least a week in orbit and let's see how quickly we can take advantage of this."

"I have clothes permanently stored on the station, sir," Collin smiled now. "I've taken the liberty of starting things in motion, so we'll be ready to board a shuttle in about ninety minutes and I will start making calls now."

"Go," Eduardo motioned him off.

Collin made it to the door as Eduardo considered the sun just finally rising now.

"Sir?" Collin asked, pausing. "What does it all mean?"

"It means that the future has just arrived, Collin," Eduardo smiled. "And that doing the little things to help people occasionally pays off in a huge way. We need to leverage this to possibly finally creating a full government for Yisan and start acting like grownups."

Collin nodded and vanished.

Eduardo considered the situation and wondered if he needed to install Collin as Yisan's first governor.

Oluchi and Fernanda, and more to the point, Grace and Lazarus, had started a revolution, after all.

SEVEN

ADDISON

"TIME TO EMERGENCE?" Addison asked as he sat and tried to not shiver with nerves as he thought about all the craziness that lay ahead.

"*Thirty seconds, Addison,*" Cormac responded quickly.

Addison nodded and gripped a little harder at his cone, wishing that maybe he'd brought Wybert with him, just in case they needed to use the guns. *Star of Kilri* was extremely heavily armed, but he also knew that using those guns for anything but last minute self-defense against real pirates would blow his cover completely.

At least he would have Lazarus and Wybert and Kuei handy if something did go wrong.

He'd never been to Oton Mari, so all Addison had to go on were the standard notes that Innruld Security maintained. However, those were a little frightening, once he had gotten into them and started reading the secrets that the masters of the galaxy didn't want shared with the lesser species.

Like him.

Just one more reason to blow the whole damned thing up, set the ruins on fire, and hunt the survivors.

Around them, the pearlescent blues and grays of trans-space faded abruptly as the vessel returned to the universe where he had been born. There was a star in the distance, a planet close by, and the largest station Addison had ever seen afore him.

Huge. Like six of Zhoonarrim Station stuck together, and then pulled like warm taffy.

And this was where the liberation would begin. At least if he was lucky.

"*Automated hail from the station,*" Cormac announced. "*Responding.*"

"You handle piloting us into dock," Addison nodded.

So far, so good. Hopefully, there was another NavCrawler over there handling things and not an organic that might be more curious about the strange yacht sailing up to Oton Mari Station. Traffic was far heavier than he was used to as well. Aceanx, Dormell, and Zhoonarrim had all been relatively quiet systems, places where traders and transports ran a regular run to move things around.

Predictable. Non-threatening.

Nothing like Oton Mari.

"*Addison, there is a Security Pyramid nearby,*" Cormac said. "*Does that change any of our plans?*"

"It does not," Addison decided. "Lazarus is already out there somewhere, so they will be prepared. And I know what the Kirov Lance did to *Gotland*. A Pyramid represents no threat to them. Presumably then, none to us."

"*As you expect,*" Cormac replied.

Now Addison was happy that Wybert wasn't here. That the goofball Ilount warrior was aboard a fighting ship. They had planned to liberate Oton Mari already. If they could kill a Security Pyramid along the way, that would just be one step closer to liberating all the Species Underground from Innruld control.

One fewer security ship Addison's rage and vengeance would have to hunt down through trans-space.

"We are being hailed by an Innruld officer now," Cormac spoke up.

"Main screen and conference mode," Addison replied. "Everyone else remain quiet."

The female face that appeared was coldly beautiful in the way of scaleless bipeds. Enormously tall and lean. Addison had spent much time around Humans to appreciate that Innruld were a foot taller on average, and yet only weighed the same.

In the past, that great height had let them intimidate the shorter species. Addison was done being intimidated. Plus, Lazarus liked to refer to the Innruld as pretty space elves in the face of an orc invasion. Having read a little Human literature, Addison wasn't sure that Lazarus was wrong with that assumption.

But today he was a wealthy dilettante seeing the galaxy in a private yacht. Not a threat to the Innruld, Your Honor.

Promise.

"Star of Kilri, we do not have a record of your vessel calling at Oton Mari before," the woman stated bluntly, but Addison had a lifetime of experience lying to the overlords.

"We have never been this far around the ring," Addison replied with all the lassitude of a rich dilettante.

"The ring?" she asked, now a little thrown off.

"I made a bet with some others, back on Gowook," Addison smiled with eyes and scales. "That we could sail the entire outer ring of Innruld Space. Every system touching on the darkness. And do it in a single year. Apparently, it has never been done before, so I can add another navigation record to the books."

Those blue-gold eyes blinked, and then a second time.

"What is your name?" she asked.

"Tountoun," Addison smiled coldly at her, trying to look down a non-existent nose at her like the bipeds did. "Addley Tountoun."

Addison wondered if all Churquen looked alike to an Innruld. It was a terrible, rude thing to say, but the number of Innruld that it did not apply to he could probably count on his fingers, not even needing some biped with toes to help out.

Thus, the liberation.

Those eyes flashed down now, certainly looking up such a name for outstanding warrants. As if one of the best-known scions of the single wealthiest Churquen clan on Gowook would have the law after him.

Unlike, say, Addison Wolcott, suspected smuggler and wanted pirate.

She looked up after a moment and her eyes got a little bigger.

"Welcome to Oton Mari, Mr. Tountoun," she said in a far less combative tone. "We do not have a VIP section where you could dock."

"Nor did I expect one," Addison replied with a superior smile. Predatory and cold, like she deserved. "After all, we are clear out on the edge of known space."

And thus, the tail end of beyond, socially as well as culturally, but he didn't say that.

"Any of the unused cargo docks will be fine," Addison continued. "We are not hauling any cargo, but will want to take on consumables at some point."

"Very good," she said, stopping herself from calling him *sir* but only barely.

She cut the line and Addison did the same before blowing out a heavy breath and finally relaxing. A Security Pyramid greatly upped the stakes, but also suggested that things were even more out of control here than he might have hoped.

Lazarus could put that to use.

EIGHT

EHA

EHA HAD SEEN this system before, but it was amazing what a few months' work could do to transform it. The station appeared complete and operational, but Eha imagined that such would have been the very first order of business, having captured it from Westphalia three-quarters done.

The three escort warships that had accompanied *Ajax* originally were still present, along with a semi-random mishmash of other military vessels, from the things Captain Nguema had been muttering under his breath during their final approach.

Eha and the Gnashiiley Captain were aboard one of his shuttles, along with Erlyn, Alla, and a few of Carlos's crew. They had just turned sideways up against an airlock and clunked loudly as everything took hold.

Carlos smiled at her and gestured for two of his marines to take escort positions at the inner part of the airlock. There had been, to quote Carlos, "a bit of a shitshow" when *Dutra* emerged from jump, informing the local authorities that he would shortly be escorting a group of alien vessels that would be landing on the planet below and establishing a small colony.

The governor, at least, was still Chief Elena Garcia who had been originally assigned to *Recife* before transferring over to *Ajax* for the battle to liberate Vilga's Stand. And Xiuying Bălan had remained as Chief of Security, so she had been able to see her friends on the comm and assure them that everything was on the up and up.

High Councilor Erlyn Teixeira was something of an afterthought, but she had put everyone on notice that this was an officially-sanctioned colonization, at least as far as that went, so they had fallen into line.

The airlock opened and the two marines stepped out onto the deck. Eha waited a long beat and then followed. Most of the folks lined up across the way were people she knew, so she smiled and slithered right over to Garcia.

"Good afternoon, Governor," Eha said.

Elena lit up with a warm, inner fire, but she had been a long-serving engineering chief, a non-commissioned officer who had more or less been struck by lightning to be promoted to a point at which her eventual retirement would be much nicer than she might have ever imagined. Similarly, Xiuying had already retired once, but now was filling in the slot for a senior officer, apparently earning more points and prestige.

Certainly, he looked better now than he had six months ago. Trimmer. Happier, even, but Eha supposed that no longer being a bouncer in a dead-end bar on Yisan might have had something to do with that. Then again, it might not, considering Xiuying.

"Good afternoon, Ambassador," Elena replied. "And welcome home, if I understand the politics of the thing correctly."

Rather than settle for the Human handshake, Eha stretched into the woman for a hug. And Xiuying as well.

It was nice having friends. For too long, she had been running agents and double agents, everyone suspect and nobody trusted.

Eha got presented to various officers from the many vessels in close proximity, including Commander Rodriguez who had been there with them before, and his two companion directors.

A reception followed, much nicer than any of the ones the High Council had thrown for her when Eha was back on Brasilia, but there she had been an alien.

Here, she was among friends. And folks wanting to be her friend.

Several hours later, she found herself finally in a smaller conference room. Erlyn, Alla, and Carlos had accompanied her, as had Elena and Xiuying.

"So you have obviously been somewhat successful," Elena said seriously, sipping at a glass of water cut with some sort of citrus that Eha found interesting enough to have gotten her own. "Now what?"

"Shortly, there will be a convoy of vessels of Innruld origin," Eha began. "Refugees from Gowook, when we broke the Innruld's control long enough for them to flee and rendezvous later."

Elena turned to Carlos and Erlyn now, a hint of terror in her eyes, but Eha understood. A year ago, this woman had been an engineer, and now she was a politician, called upon to make decisions far beyond her pay grade, with no obvious right answer.

Well, there was one right answer always. Fall back on the Founding of the Rio Alliance itself.

*"Quando no curso de eventos
Humanos…"*
*"When in the course of Human
events…"*

The Alliance itself was a statement of principles for all alien species to live in peace and harmony, regardless of what those eggless Westphalian bastards on Earth thought. Elena was on safe enough ground assuming that the Founding also covered Churquen, Yithadreph, and the few other species represented.

Still…

"Councilor?" Elena asked nervously. "Captain?"

"You will be operating under my authority, Governor," Councilor Teixeira said formally. "Captain Nguema is following civilian orders—my orders—to resettle these refugees at 6357 Wei Xiu IV, in the system commonly referred to as Vilga's Stand. They have surveyed the records and have requested a reservation claim roughly eleven miles long by nine, along a certain river and extending to roughly half of the bay where the river debauches into the sea. Representing the High Council, I have approved the request, subject to subsequent surveys on the ground."

"Is that enough?" Xiuying spoke up now, looking more like a military officer than Eha remembered. "Will that be large enough over the longer term?"

If she was reading the signs correctly, he had also been spending sufficient time around Elena Garcia that they seemed to have some level of personal relationship as well.

"For now we believe so," Alla replied. "The total population at this moment is just under four thousand, most of whom are accustomed to living in an urban center. We will build the core of a new city, along with roads, parks, and farmland, and then infiltrate your biosphere with galumphs."

Eha snickered at the way her mother described it, but without predators, they would breed in a manner similar to Human rabbits. She wondered how long it would be for the native predators to adapt to eating such creatures.

"Infiltrate, madam?" Elena asked, more nervous.

"Livestock raised for food, Elena," Eha leaned in before anyone else said anything. "Small, stupid, and herbivorous, but they will escape any pens eventually and breed in the wild. They do that everywhere they have been seeded."

"Dangerous?" Xiuying spoke up.

"Terran Rabbits," Carlos laughed. "I actually got to hold one when I had the same question. Six legs instead of four. About as dumb as goats, but nowhere near as mean."

"Oh, okay," Xiuying nodded. "Good eating?"

"We'll have a barbecue one of these days to celebrate our freedom," Eha laughed, having picked up a number of Human customs over the period she had been in such close proximity to them.

"One question," Erlyn Teixeira turned serious and looked right at Eha. "How quickly can we build a complete, sophisticated, and proper hospital as part of the new city?"

"Why is that first?" Elena asked, getting nervous again. "I appreciate that people can live a little rough while they put down homes and such, but why is a hospital first order of business?"

Eha blushed. To Humans, it was all the scales around her chin and eyes flaring away from the skin, where a Human's face turned red.

"What's your estimate, Eha?" Erlyn asked.

"About two months," Alla replied when Eha froze.

"So in about two months, the colony will have its first birth, Governor," Erlyn smiled. "And it will be an important one, so I want every medical facility available in place."

Xiuying turned to her and Eha felt her flares double again.

"Addison knows, then?" he asked.

"Everyone but you knew," Eha smiled. "He sent me here, with my mother, so we could raise the young one free. But I will not remain that long afterwards, most likely, so Alla will be the Governor of the colony."

"I wouldn't be too sure about that, Eha," Erlyn smiled now. It was a wicked smile, but Eha had come to understand the woman, and knew that Teixeira would be playing a game on someone else.

"Oh?"

"I'm going to have to coordinate a great many things from here," she said "So I'm going to send a messenger to Brasilia and ask the entire High Council to come here. This is where the next stage of the Rio Alliance is going to be decided."

Elena took a deep enough breath that everyone turned to her now.

"Does this new colony have a name yet?" she asked. "Yesterday, it was just a system, but tomorrow it will become someone's home."

"Indeed it does," Eha replied, nodding to Erlyn. "With the Council's tentative approval, we're going to call it Liberty."

NINE

EDUARDO

SCOUTWALL, not GunWall. Eduardo had to remind himself that the Westphalian squadron had been part of a ScoutWall, sent into the Nebula to locate the aliens. And they had, at least to a certain extent.

More importantly, they had, however briefly, found the elusive *Ajax*, parked in orbit while Lazarus and friends had gone…on. Had then fought a battle against the Rio Alliance Patrol Cruiser *Dutra*, which was the vessel that Lieutenant Marie Oslor had been on before Lazarus had sent her here, as well as an apparently captured Innruld vessel.

The Rio contingent consisted of six crew members: three officers and three chiefs, but it was obvious to Eduardo that Oslor was the important player, even as junior as she might be ranked. She had known Addison Wolcott, who was still a mystery to Eduardo, even as central as the Churquen captain had become.

Once the Westphalians had been loaded aboard two chartered vessels—really semi-retired cruise ships—and sent off, Eduardo had called upon Lt. Oslor. Just him, Collin, and Marie.

They were aboard his station. She was staying at a hotel he owned. The woman was a little overwhelmed by the luxury, but he wasn't here to seduce her body. Mind, perhaps, but that was a different story entirely. She had clues he needed.

"And from there, Admiral da Silva and Captain Oliveira took their ransom and instructed me to deliver the crews to you for their repatriation and the ships for disposal, sir," Marie said, finishing her tale.

It was an impressive story. She was an impressive woman, especially as he had grandchildren her age and he had a hard time thinking of them as adults.

When had he gotten old?

Marie Oslor was dark-skinned, as was normal in the Rio Alliance, when so many colonists this far out had originally come from South America on Earth, rather than the northern regions. Black hair. Attractive. Collin certainly seemed to find her extremely attractive, but Eduardo suspected the man might be smitten by her ability to boil down a complex report that would be several thousand pages of details and appendices, and only provide the cogent points in a coherent, well-threaded narrative.

But Collin was like that.

"Did either man say what you were to do with the excess funds, Lieutenant?" Eduardo asked.

"They did, sir, but I'm not sure I understand," Marie said hesitantly. "Captain Oliveira told me that you, or whoever I dealt with, should *bank them against future trade imbalances.*"

Eduardo heard Collin's tiny gasp and smiled. It was something of a technical term that not many people would understand, outside of interstellar finance. Lazarus was, in a quiet way, establishing a bank of commerce on Yisan that the aliens from Innruld Space could call upon for loans.

Facilitating trade by assuring the finance people on Yisan that there was money available.

Lazarus was telling Eduardo and friends in no uncertain terms that there would be such significant trade flowing into and through Yisan that a bank of that scale was going to be necessary, and he was getting Westphalia to finance it, however unwillingly.

"Sir?" Marie asked, perhaps a bit nervous at the reaction she was getting.

"Political and diplomatic concerns, Lieutenant," he assured her. "You have not met my Ambassador on Brasilia, Oluchi Pryce, who could have explained it all. Suffice it to say that everything is well. Now, how may I assist you and your team in getting where you need to go next?"

She hesitated, and Eduardo smiled at her in a disarming way. After all, he had just officially called Pryce a representative. Hard to disown the man at a later date, although there were always ways.

"From here, I was instructed to make my way to Vilga's Stand if I could, sir," Marie explained. "*Dutra* was headed there with the convoy and hopefully I can rejoin before they head back to Innruld Space."

Eduardo felt something lurch. He'd missed some key detail, overlooked perhaps in focusing on the wrong thing?

"Convoy?" he repeated the word.

"*Dutra* is escorting a convoy of refugee ships from Innruld Space, sir," Marie nodded. "Taking them directly to the fourth world at 6357 Wei Xiu, where they are apparently going to establish a colony. Mostly Churquen and Yithadreph, from what I understand."

"Eha and Aileen," Eduardo breathed. He paused so briefly that Collin might be the only person that noticed. "Good news, then, Lieutenant Oslor."

"Sir?"

"I will be able to transport you and your team directly there from here," he decided. "I will need to meet with Ambassador Dunham again, and possibly High Councilor Teixeira to work out some details."

He turned to Collin and caught the man's nod. Just like that, it would happen, as soon as a ship could be identified, prepared, and loaded. Just another reason Collin would go far in this organization.

He started to say more when a signal chimed.

"I have an urgent message for Eduardo Martìnez," the woman's recorded voice said.

Eduardo grimaced, but the systems were supposed to only respond to certain things. Someone had said the right words, and the computer was responding. Whoever it was had best hope they hadn't overstepped their bounds or he might have to chastise them later.

"Go ahead," he said, after a quick glance at an extremely nervous Lieutenant Marie Oslor, in machinations well over her head but maintaining a calm face on things.

The system chimed again.

"This is Martìnez," he said, maybe a little grumpy.

"Good afternoon, sir," the happy voice replied. "This is Oluchi Pryce, with Fernanda Flores and Anya Persaud along. We've just arrived in-system and I was hoping you might be able to make some time to be briefed."

Pryce? Here? With Fernanda? Was it exceptionally good, or had all hell broken loose, back on Brasilia? They would not be aware of the battle that *Ajax* and *Dutra* had won on the edge of Innruld Space, so he had to hope it was the former.

You could never read anything in Oluchi Pryce's eyes or voice. Certainly not across a poker table, and diplomatic negotiations would be an exceptionally high stakes version.

"I'm in orbit on Platform Prime, Pryce," he replied. "Have whoever route you here directly. Time is of the essence at both ends, so move quick and prepare to continue."

"Understood, sir," the man replied. "We can brief you in route to wherever, as you are obviously more up to date on things than I am."

"I doubt that, Oluchi," Eduardo laughed. "But we will both benefit. I will talk to you shortly. System, cut the line."

It chimed again at the room felt smaller. Again, the quick nod from Collin that he could adjust plans that were less than five minutes old and already wrong, but that was the sort of thing that happened as you got down to signing a major deal with that many moving parts.

"Is everything still good, sir?" Marie asked.

"It is, Lieutenant," he nodded. "You will more likely be privy to the sorts of things that get written up in history books, if all goes well."

"If you say so, sir," she nodded.

"I will leave you to update your people, Marie," Eduardo said as he rose. "We will let you know as soon as we have a departure window, but it should be less than a day, so you should best prepare."

"Understood, sir."

And then he and Collin were in the hallway, Collin already on the comm making arrangements. Eduardo started sending messages as well. Leena Hernández would need to be in on this, as she was probably second behind him in terms of total wealth with Ardna's organization still in turmoil and probate.

They would be heading to a place where Innruld refugees were already being settled, so he had missed his first opportunity, but Eduardo also understood that Lazarus could have sent Marie Oslor to a Rio Alliance base just as easily, and he would have been months behind the curve by the time the information caught up with him.

Because he needed move, ***right now***, if he wished to be at the table when the victors began dividing the spoils of war.

TEN

OLUCHI

OLUCHI LOOKED around the thing Eduardo had called a yacht. Technically, he was probably correct, only because somewhere, someone had expanded the definition of such a thing to include a vessel four hundred feet long, seventy feet at the widest, and five full decks.

With an enormous crew.

Where else would you have Ambassadorial Suites numbered, anyway?

But he was forward at the bow now, in a space possibly originally designed as a medium-sized dance hall. The group rattled hollowly around, but Eduardo had moved them all to a smaller table in a corner so they could talk. And maybe have a full halftime show behind them later if they needed the break.

There was room for it.

Eduardo was a fabulous host, putting down a fantastic spread for lunch that put Fernanda's chef a bit to shame, but Oluchi wasn't about to tell anyone that. Well, maybe whisper it in Anya's ear when they were all sweaty and snuggling.

Lunch was done and cleared. He was opposite Eduardo and

Leena, between Anya and Fernanda, diagonal from Collin Lau, watching Rio Alliance Lieutenant Oslor. She was the one who was out of place here, but only because she'd come from a blue collar background like he had and didn't have the extra twenty-five years experience of learning how to quietly fit into this scene.

"Will Rio truly allow Ms. Dunham's people to settle there?" Collin was asking now, looking mostly at Oluchi, for reasons that were possibly the most frightening.

Oluchi Pryce, Deputy Ambassador from the Species Underground to the Rio Alliance. The title held a kernel of truth. He'd been the point man, fencing with Cavalcanti and the rest, dickering about trade percentages, bonding warehouses, and currency conversions, as weird as that might be.

He might have learned a few things sitting at a poker table with dangerous players like Eduardo.

"It appears so," Oluchi temporized. "Lt. Oslor has been closer to the center of that decision-making than I have."

"Marie."

"Pardon?" he asked as he turned to the woman.

"Please, call me Marie," she repeated. "I am mostly off duty until I get back to my ship, so Lieutenant Oslor feels strange, when all of you are on a first name basis."

"Marie," he nodded before turning to the rest. "Most of you have met Lazarus and Eha. Erlyn Teixeira is a sharp operator, so she saw the advantage to settling refugees, doubly so with the symbolism of Vilga's Stand, which was originally such a famous battle that even I was aware of it."

"What will Westphalia do in response?" Leena spoke up now.

Of all of them, she was perhaps the greatest outsider, but only because Oluchi knew the rest better. Leena was the daughter and widow of two different shipping houses, and perhaps close to Eduardo for net value, although most of hers was tied up in family real estate holdings and art collections rather than outright ownership of cash-bearing companies like that man.

Her face had aged in the last year, almost to the point that she reminded Oluchi of a rail thin scarecrow, one possessed of strange tastes and fetishes. Leena had generally liked it rougher in bed than most of the men or women Oluchi had known, which was just another reason he had preferred an adventurous, outdoorsy woman like Fernanda.

"When word gets out, I expect that the specists in charge on Earth will probably try their luck again in taking the system," Oluchi mused. "They will need more force next time, with a fully operational defensive station in orbit, but that's nothing that cannot be overcome. The Rio High Command will need to permanently station a significant naval force there to protect it, and Admiral Santos has told me on more than one occasion that he didn't immediately have those forces available. But that was before. Times have changed."

"They have indeed," Eduardo said, eyes locking on him now and then turning to study Anya, as if he could pierce her shell and study the spy underneath.

Ex-spy? Oluchi wasn't entirely sure.

It was complicated seemed to be his motto anyway, so there was no reason not to extend that to her.

She was possibly Erlyn's agent. Possibly someone else's. His lover, and a woman doing a good job convincing him that she was on his side. Now, she had to convince the most dangerous person at the table of that as well.

Oluchi might have actually killed more people, or at least been present when others had done the killing, but he didn't figure Eduardo for a slouch in that department. The only question was really how long ago had the most recent victim been?

"You are an operative, Anya," Eduardo stated.

"I am that, as well, sir," she agreed. "Right now, I wish to be involved on the business side of things for all the same reasons that you are, Eduardo."

"And that is?"

"A new colony is an opportunity to build an entire economic and industrial infrastructure," Anya replied. "That requires a lot of investment, but promises significant returns. This will be the first truly alien colony in Human Space, so these will be the relationships that determine the future of the Rio Alliance and shape all its interactions with the soon-to-be-former Innruld Space. That is a lot of zeroes, and I would like my chance to perhaps earn some of that, just as Oluchi is doing."

Eduardo studied her closely. Reading her soul, as Oluchi's sainted mother might have described it. Weighing it, if nothing else.

The man smiled, so hopefully he saw some of the same things Oluchi did. But he'd examined her at a much closer range than merely across a dining table. (Oluchi had also had the woman on a few conference tables. Anya was, after all, something of an exhibitionist.)

But they were serious now. The fun could come later.

"Who is it you work for?" Eduardo asked baldly, ignoring the gasps and grunts of disapproval around the table.

"Erlyn Teixeira," she replied, just as flatly. "And the Alliance Block on the High Council, as much as that group has a formal structure. I was a deep cover agent for several years, buried in the planning department where I could take the pulse of the organization and see things that never bubbled up out of the civil service."

"And now?" Eduardo pressed.

"My cover is completely and irrevocably blown, Eduardo," she focused on him, even as a hand found Oluchi's under the table for strength. "I will certainly be retired by the agency and put out to pasture at thirty-six standard years, so now I have to find out what I want to do with the rest of my life."

"Depending on how one might interpret it, Oluchi Pryce works for me," Eduardo smiled, glancing his way briefly. "At least that's what he had been telling people to get their attention."

"And Fernanda dropped a major bomb on Rio by suggesting that Yisan and some of your associated worlds might go so far as to ally with the Rio Alliance, or even join it, if the price was right."

"Would it compromise your ethics to be involved in those negotiations from the other side of the table?" Eduardo asked now, dropping his own bomb on the woman.

Oluchi wondered if she could actually squeeze his hand any harder right now.

"I do not believe so," Anya answered slowly, carefully. "As long as certain things remained unknown by you. Mostly dates and blackmail material that should remain buried."

"I find that a useful starting point," Eduardo nodded. He turned to Collin Lau then, and gestured with his head.

"There is a proposal in place," Collin began in perfectly clear diction. "It would formalize a manner of republican government for the Yisan system, using a classical tripartite structure. We suspect that it would also become a template for many of our allied worlds, when they decide to consider the same things as Eduardo's organization has planned."

"And that would be?" Oluchi asked, figuring he could be the straight man here.

"Forming, at a minimum, a new stellar association that would for now become a third nation," Collin turned to him.

"Westphalia. The Rio Alliance. Yisan plus friends, whatever we end up calling it."

Oluchi felt the gravity in the room tip over for a long moment before it righted itself.

"And Innruld, whatever they end up calling that," Oluchi replied.

"We are closer to Rio than Westphalia," Eduardo spoke up. "Physically as well as socially. Possibly closer to Innruld than either, although we will not know for sure until treaties are signed and wars fought."

"This might mean war with Westphalia, Eduardo," Oluchi pointed out.

"It might," the man nodded grimly. "Best we be prepared, then, isn't it?"

ELEVEN

LAZARUS

LAZARUS HAD INTERVIEWED Ereshkiki Nisab and Kuei extensively on Innruld technology before he had attempted this. He knew exactly how far that station's scanners could tell that *Ajax* was something other than an asteroid quietly adrift in the distance.

Humans would have trained any number of optical telescopes on the object after passive scans detected it, but the Innruld did not foster curiosity the same way. Crushed it, whenever necessary, except for those things that could enhance Innruld power and control.

Nobody would do more than mark a potential navigational hazard in the logs and be done. They would not be compelled to just sail out for the privilege of saying that they had been the first to stand on an alien rock.

Another thing that marked the two cultures so radically different. But he could work with it. Take advantage of it.

"Helm, what is your status?" Lazarus asked, just to break up the long silence as folks watched and didn't do much.

"One hundred and seventy-four ships in close proximity to the station, Captain," Kuei answered, mostly by rote.

There wasn't much to do out here except be prepared to come to the rescue if something happened to Addison.

The hatch behind him opened and Lazarus glanced back to see Aileen approaching.

"Clock says you are supposed to go take a nap," she announced in a sarcastic tone, whiskers all the way forward to make her point. "Second Officer has the watch now."

Lazarus caught Kuei's snicker and rose.

"Got time to chat?" he asked Aileen, gesturing to the day watch office where someone would be doing paperwork, if they had a full crew consuming foodstuffs and needing to sit qualifying exams and recertifications.

"Expecting trouble?" she snarked up at him and turned the other direction.

"I'm never expecting it," Lazarus replied as he followed her into the smaller room and closed the door. "But it does have a habit of following me around from time to time."

"I've noticed," she grinned, walking around the desk and climbing up into the chair that had been drilled and polished to add a tail hole. "Short of blowing everything up, like we did at Gowook, what's there to do?"

Lazarus took the seat on this side and stretched out. This one was designed for Humans. There were several others collapsed in a corner that had been designed for every other method of biological construction he might encounter, which had given Thadrakho great joy to build.

"At some point, we will have to blow things up," he reminded her. "The Innruld will not willingly cede power to the Species Underground. Not after so long. And they are not smart enough to understand what Humanity means to their ongoing control of these sectors of space."

Her whiskers flared backwards now, but he was expecting that. Aileen was a specialist in cargo, not a trained killer like him. None of the Species did violence like a Human did.

Like all Humans did.

"Do we just hammer them into the mud right now?" Lazarus asked her. "Make an example of Oton Mari and start tearing everything down before Westphalia or da Silva's people return?"

He watched her eyes get a little big, but then grimness set in.

"There aren't enough big guns available," she replied after a moment of deep thought. "Metallurgy is pretty good for hulls. Shields still suck comparatively. But you'll need big guns to make your point. More than we have back in storage, too. Maybe we need to take an industrial facility and have it start turning out basic Rio Star Spears and Lances? Piracy will get ugly, but that's going to come out of Innruld's hide, and not ours. Rio ships will just stomp on the pirates if they have to. Westphalia as well, but they won't know what to expect and will likely get themselves into a shooting war with the Species. Best start that as soon as possible."

Lazarus was a little surprised at the ferocity of her words and tone, but Aileen had changed at least as much as he had over the last year or so. They had both grown more serious.

The *Star of Kilri* was much more heavily armed than anything else it would encounter, because da Silva had brought spare guns with him on *Dutra* the first time.

"So what will you say when da Silva wants to put you in command of another warship?" Lazarus asked. It was only partly teasing because Rod had mentioned it privately, mostly to see what he thought on the topic.

"You'll all learn some ripe new profanities," she growled.

But Lazarus knew she would step up if he asked. Would take that step and become another command officer, if only because they would need people they could trust in charge of things.

There was likely to be a lot of shooting when the hammer finally fell.

TWELVE

ADDISON

THE AREA where *Star of Kilri* docked wasn't that impressive, but Addison had been warned. Oton Mari didn't get toffs around here, looking for the best food and entertainment. The locals were miners, who tended to be a much rougher lot. It was a good thing Addison wasn't really a wealthy dilettante, or they might have been a bit of trouble.

As it was, he crossed the deck with Remahle along as something of a bodyguard. Just a Churquen and a Kr'mari out for a stroll, but that also kept anyone from easily sneaking up on him. Addison had added a holster from *Ajax*'s stores and put a Manticore light laspistol in it. His hands weren't big enough for something like the Ares that Lazarus preferred.

For once in his life, Addison even missed having Wybert along. Not the old goofball, slightly soft in the head but the new Wybert, who had trained in Japanese spear combat under Xiuying and then watched a lot of videos. He was almost Human now, in his martial skills repertoire.

Oton Mari Control had at least docked Addison away from the strip of shops and bars where most of the miners were. Back in a place where supplies got delivered to the station and broken down for delivery to individual shops.

Quiet. Dirty and worn, but that was entropy and not malice.

He slithered intentionally across the deck towards a specific tea shop. Remahle waddled along in his wake.

The place was again more of a local pub than a miner bar. But that was by design. On Zhoonarrim or Dormell, it would have been the sort of place where directors and bankers met, but most of the mining vessels had a crew of one or two, rather than a large group like *Shiva Zephyr Glaive*.

The keeper behind the bar was a Zentra. Male, as the red feathers covering the body were highlighted with both black and white feathers. He was a little taller than H'Brige Slani, but not as broad across the torso, nor did he have the seven-fan tail of an Atomarsk.

Addison nodded and made his way to a table. Remahle picked out a chair he could use as a perch and climbed atop it.

"Citizens," the Zentra nodded as he approached, delivering menus for them and departing.

Addison drew a quiet breath clear to the tip of his tail and considered his options. The food would be fairly generic. The teas were all carefully marked for ingredients. But that wasn't why he was nervous. They had made it this far, into a place that might be the next step in the revolution.

At his regular shipping calls, he had a network of folks he knew and trusted from long association. Members of the Species Underground that Eha had recruited and vouched for.

Here, he had nothing but a set of codewords and signals to contact such an organization, and the hope that it hadn't been penetrated and destroyed at some point.

If it was a trap, at least he had a mob of crazed Humans who could come rescue him, but that was such a terrible outcome that Addison hoped it would never be necessary.

They waited and eventually the keeper returned to take their orders for food and tea.

"Now what?" Remahle asked after they were alone.

"We wait," Addison murmured. "We are being observed, hopefully, but they will have no greater trust of us than we of them."

"Is the Pyramid outside a problem?" Remahle's mind was flitting all over the place, but he was a Kr'mari, and the glider squirrels tended to be like that.

"If it is, *Ajax* will handle it," Addison reassured him, hoping that he wasn't lying.

But then, Addison had seen *Ajax* kill much more dangerous things than a mere Security Pyramid.

He reached into a pouch now and withdrew some paper cash to pay for the bill, along with a slip of paper that had a random-looking doodle on it. Placing the pile on the table between them with the extra note tucked in, he settled on his coil and watched the others in here, wondering who might be members of the Underground or Innruld spies.

Addison had no great interest in shooting his way out of this bar, but that wasn't the same as being unprepared. Remahle had a little stunner in a pouch, but he was not prepared if things went sideways.

Time passed. The keeper returned with tea and collected the pile of money and papers without comment.

Now, they would see. Addison could not move quickly, but then neither could about half the species he knew. Humans were the fastest over long distances, because they had such terribly-dangerous endurance. Aknaan and Innruld were probably the quickest over short sprints. But Addison had a Rio Alliance comm in a pouch and could always summon the apocalypse down upon this station if it became necessary.

It was as though his heart was echoing clear through to the tip of his tail, but that was just nerves wanting to panic, even as he sat on his coil and tried to pretend that this was just another lunch out with one of his crew.

The keeper returned with plates. Battered and pan-fried galumph strips for him. Salad with shrimp for Remahle. The man set everything down and then dug change out of a pocket, placing it exactly back on the table with a different piece of paper tucked in. Addison ignored it except to leave a tip and tuck the rest into a pouch. If this was legitimate, someone would follow him and eventually make contact, presumably back at the ship.

If not—…well, there was always Lazarus and his people.

Addison focused on eating. It had been forever since he had eaten galumph strips, and might be a while again.

He felt eyes on his scales, but nobody was gazing this way when he looked up.

However, Addison was certain he had started something.

THIRTEEN

EHA

PLANETFALL. So different from Gowook. Heavier, but Eha would get used to it. Innruld worlds tended to be lighter in gravity and everything related than the Humans preferred, but they could all live together here.

The sky overhead was more blue than red or green, but this was an oceanic world, more than fifty percent covered with salt water. The Human homeworld was apparently something like seventy percent, but she had no interest in visiting, at least not while the Westphalian government was hostile to aliens. But if Rio won the war, what would that mean?

Dreams for future days, to carry her child there sometime.

They had landed all of the ships a little inland from where the city would be built, in an area tentatively marked by Addison for a starport. Governor Garcia's station was geo-synched not exactly overhead, but permanently about thirty degrees above the horizon from here, so it would always be a star in the night, moving against the others.

Several pinckes were on the ground as well from *Dutra*

and the station, bringing half as many Humans down as aliens walking and slithering around. Most folks were concentrating on building the first warehouses and temporary living quarters for the port itself, so Carlos had brought down a pair of wheeled combat transports. They were not all that comfortable to ride in, but at least Eha had been able to wrap the bottom of her tail around a chair and her mother was next to her.

Eha felt like a balloon about to burst, but this was no time to stop all the things she was doing. She had mere weeks before the little one would arrive, supposedly. And stubborn didn't at all run in either family.

The vehicle pulled to a stop on a small rise that had a good view of a kink in the river that almost formed a peninsula, like a tail stuck into the water.

"Here?" Carlos asked, just to confirm.

"Here," Alla spoke before Eha could.

Two Churquen joined over a dozen Humans in a wide meadow. This planet was relatively young, as planets went. There had been life when the first explorers found it, but nothing more sophisticated than lichen. Humans had brought in plants and bacteria first, adding ecosystems of animals later, as well as letting things reorganize themselves.

There were predators about that had no fear of Humans or Churquen, but Carlos had armed marines around a perimeter, as well as sensors on the two trucks watching and listening.

Alla turned to her now with an appraising look. Her mother's way of telling Eha to get her tail to slithering. Instead of moving, Eha spun slowly in place once.

The land here was a little higher on this side of the river, which was part of the reason they had chosen it. Floods would hit the lowlands on the other side more frequently. At the same time, trees and meadows had mixed well, but that was the century since everything had been planted and left to grow. It wasn't a mature planet they were visiting.

And she would be adding all manner of Innruld bacteria and lifeforms to the Human mix, creating something entirely new. Hopefully good.

Eha found the spot she wanted and slithered slowly along the line her keel identified as the ridgeline itself, a sinuous curve that roughly followed the river below, and perhaps represented an earlier flood plain, millions of years ago.

There was a peak here as well. Not much. Perhaps an entire body length over several hundred yards, but enough of one. Eha turned to Carlos, finding that he had moved right along in behind her and was holding a long metal stake in one hand. He handed it to her and Eha found the spot she wanted to drive it into the ground.

Another Human invention. The Innruld didn't need anything like this, because they dictated the rules to everyone else and you dealt with it or they put you in a prison camp until you saw the error of your ways.

This thing she was holding was a pipe. Eha depressed the first button and it telescoped out to more than six feet in length. She rested the pointed end into the soil and stood it upright before pressing the second button. A motor inside spun up and Eha felt it right itself gyroscopically before beginning to corkscrew itself into the ground to a depth of three feet.

A red light on the tip blinked every second and a half for visual sensors and optically-based creatures to notice.

"Zero, zero," Carlos said in a voice that seemed louder than usual. "Welcome home."

But then, she had just established the baseline coordinate system for this entire planet, with a magnetic north close to the axis of rotation. They were in what would become the southern hemisphere as these things were measured. All longitude and latitude lines would emerge from here.

She turned to the Gnashiiley and found her mother coiled up beside him and Erlyn on the other side. Around them, the Humans kept watch.

Eha pointed with her arms directly out sideways.

"I think that we should put a market square here, with the space on the left organized for the government complex we'll need to build eventually, and the hospital on the right," Eha announced to them, making it more or less official. "We can run a road right along here, with wharves and docks below and farms a little upriver. But we can start here."

It would be good, damn it. The Species would be free. Eha didn't care what the Innruld or Westphalia thought.

FOURTEEN

GORE

SEATED COMFORTABLY in his private room at the club, Gore Wescott was proud of himself. He had managed to keep most of his organization intact, after all the problems that had arisen with the arrival of the aliens. Periodic investigations by Rio's spymasters had not uncovered him or his agents, even when they had managed to track some of the things he had done and thwart more than one of them from moving forward.

Nobody in a position to know who Gore was had been suspected, and those taken had all been isolated. Pawns sacrificed for position, but not critical to the game itself.

Westphalia had been warned about *Ajax* and the aliens. Presumably, they had sent ships to investigate, but something had gone wrong. Terribly, horribly awry, because he was reading a report, brought to him just now by Benedict Spearing, indicating that aliens had arrived at Vilga's Stand and were in the process of establishing a colony.

"How is this possible?" he hissed quietly.

The room was as secure against eavesdropping as he could

make it, but that did not make it safe. Spearing sat across from him with a look of pain on his face.

"I do not know," Benedict answered. "The information is under a seal right now, but a contact was able to pass me enough fragments to assemble something for you. We know that Dunham has returned, and somehow smuggled out an entire colony from Innruld."

"Smuggled?" Gore probed, making certain he had the right word.

"Nine vessels," Benedict nodded. "None of them armed or new, and all primitive, according to fragmentary navy reports that accompanied the info, although I have not seen the scan logs themselves. Roughly four thousand beings, mostly of the types known as Churquen and Yithadreph."

Naga and Dire Otters, to use the more common terms that had percolated up from the bureaucracy. Dangerous aliens.

Worse, harbingers of more. Billions of others somewhere, just waiting for their chance to fall upon Humanity and overrun them.

Except…

Gore flipped back to an earlier section. Starkly primitive designs. And they used a form of FTL called trans-space that was much slower than current technology.

Had the aliens come this far with hopes of being bootstrapped up to a new civilization, higher than the one they had left behind? If Innruld Space was that primitive, they would be easy to conquer.

And impossible to hold. Thousands of worlds. If nothing else, it would be a modern reenactment of the *Battle of Isandlwana*. At best, a repeat of *Rorke's Drift*.

That many aliens could simply win on attrition, if they didn't mind a mismatched casualty ratio. There would be no way to stop such a tide if they started an invasion, short of planetary xenocides, and Gore wasn't sure if his Westphalian masters would go that far.

"What are our options?" Spearing asked now in a pained voice, almost echoing the words in Gore's head.

"If they know where to find us, probably little," Gore mused. "If they are that primitive, we need to build more warships, just so they cannot overwhelm us, but that will be expensive in both time and money. Similarly, trying to conquer all those worlds risks bleeding us dry, which might be why it was so easy to leak such information."

"Sir?"

"Could you imagine Grand Fleet sailing into Innruld Space and conquering it?" Gore asked. "Easy to do, if the aliens are so weak, but we could not hold those worlds. Worse, the Grand Fleet might try, and split our forces down the center when Rio decides to strike."

"What can we do?" Spearing asked.

"We could destroy the colony, but that will be expensive." Gore considered his options. "We can let Rio bleed itself trying to rescue those savages and spend all their resources there, but that only buys us a decade at most. After that, alien warships might start appearing that are as good as ours, and in significant enough numbers to break Westphalia."

"Do we flee?" Spearing gasped.

It had always been a worst case scenario. Pack up a convoy of colony ships, much like those damnable aliens had apparently done, and vanish into the galactic depths, to return like the Dorians at a later date.

Would it be necessary?

"I am not qualified to judge," Gore finally said. "But all of the galaxy is poised on a crux right now, and it might become necessary. I would rather give up the luxury of this undercover mission for a fetid swamp than live with a Rio

Alliance victory. Doubly so if it means so many more animals pretending to be intelligent beings."

"Can nothing stop it?"

"Dunham seems to be the key right now," Gore decided. "Turn all your agents loose on locating her. If we can kill that creature, we might derail everything else long enough for the fleet to make an impact. I fear the fuse is burning."

Spearing knew him well enough to recognize a dismissal. He rose with a quick bow of his head and departed silently. The usual waitress appeared quickly with a fresh glass, as though she was reading his mind or listening at the door to know the timing.

But if the woman were actually doing that, someone would have arrested him or just shot him by now.

Gore didn't think it was all a trap. Or rather, it wasn't his.

But how was he going to save Westphalia?

FIFTEEN

ADDISON

ADDISON WAS COILED NERVOUSLY around the command station on *Kilri's* bridge, squeezing and releasing in long cycles that would probably cause him to have a headache later, but served to keep him from twitching too much right now.

It had been a few hours. Cormac was here, but he was always here and watching the bridge of whatever ship he was aboard. Addison was here because returning to his cabin wouldn't have given him a grip bar.

A signal chimed at the airlock.

If he hadn't been so tightly focused on his cone, Addison might have sprung madly into the air with a scream. He needed to relax now, if that was possible, but Addison had spent a decade as a rogue. A termite slowly eating away at the foundations of Innruld Space.

Now, he was a rebel.

"Cormac?" he asked in a breathless voice.

"*Checking,*" the NavCrawler answered calmly, like always. "*Yithadreph male. Dressed like a docker, rather than a miner. Suggestions of furtiveness about his ears and whiskers.*"

Trust Cormac to know those things, after so many years around Aileen.

Addison opened an intercom inside the ship.

"We have a visitor aft," he said. "Remahle, join me at the airlock. Everyone else stand by."

Addison untangled his tail and slithered to one side, adjusting his usual bandoleer harness and checking that the pistol was riding well. The Human pistol. The symbol of how destructive that species really was when they set their minds to it.

Addison Wolcott set his mind.

"Cormac, confirm that he is alone and then let him into the inner airlock but lock him there," Addison ordered. "I will let him out myself."

"*In process.*"

Addison headed aft. The *Star of Kilri* was a box, with two doors exiting the bridge to hallways that ran parallel aft to meet at the engine room. It could hold a crew of ten easily, all the way up to sixteen in a pinch, but he had only brought five: Ereshkiki Nisab, Thadrakho, Khyaa'sha, Remahle and the two Crawlers.

None of them were warriors, with Aileen and Wybert over on *Ajax*, so he had to handle this himself, like the ancient Human archetype of a cowboy samurai. Idly, he wondered if a hat would improve his current outfit. Or his humor.

Remahle was stationed outside the airlock when Addison arrived, stunner in one hand and pointed straight down like he had been trained. Addison considered it and went ahead and drew the Manticore, letting the cold mass center his keel on the deck and focus his mind on a high noon showdown.

Probably shouldn't have read so much Human literature, but he had wanted to understand where they came from. The legends a people tell each other are the ones that tell you who they dream of being.

Cowboy samurai and Grail Knights. Dangerous gauchos, men and women of violence, usually only when it was demanded of them, rather than the casual, unthinking brutality of their literary villains.

Addison took a deep breath and settled his scales as he reached out with his free hand and triggered the airlock door.

He wasn't exactly pointing his pistol at the stranger, but close enough to make a point about someone knocking on an airlock uninvited.

The man stood perfectly still, arms just far enough away from his body to indicate peaceful intentions. Addison studied him closely. Taller than Aileen, but with the similar, blocky build of their kind. Fur that wasn't pale so much as maybe faded, down from the nearly auburn of a Gnashiiley. The mobile face and whiskers of a furred biped, who tended to communicate with the whole face and hands, since they lacked scales and a tail.

Well, stubby tail, tucked up inside the pants where it couldn't semaphore. He wore high boots and baggy pants in dark gray, like a dock worker. White T-shirt and a dark jacket that showed stains from things where he had brushed up against a dirty shipping container.

Most importantly, the fellow was unarmed, at least visibly. Might be something tucked in, but not in hand.

"How can I help you?" Addison asked simply, going ahead and aiming the Human death ray at the Yithadreph as a statement of purpose, if not intent.

The man swallowed nervously anyway.

"Expansion," he said quietly, eyes locked in now.

Ah, a messenger. Hopefully. Or Innruld Security was trying to infiltrate. Cormac would be watching for other ships approaching, since they weren't docked internally. Only the Pyramid would be a threat to *Star of Kilri*. And then not for very long with *Ajax* nearby.

"Equal," Addison replied, starting the rhythm for two agents to identify one another.

This one was an older code, which made the risk greater that it had been cracked, but he had been gone for nearly a year now and didn't know what things were like on this side of Innruld Space.

"Surprise."

"Watch."

"Pledge," the Yithadreph said, finally relaxing some.

"Registration." Addison completed the sequence and studied his partner.

"I'm Briston Moora," the Yithadreph introduced himself with a sigh.

"Addison Wolcott," he replied. Addison backed and turned, headed into the wardroom, where they could at least all sit. "This is Remahle Mebarsu. Come."

The three of them ended up seated at the long trestle table. Cormac and Ereshkiki Nisab were no doubt listening in from either end of the boat. It wasn't safe, but it was as close as Addison figured he could get, starting from scratch in a new system.

"What brings you to Oton Mari?" Briston asked as they settled.

"Revolution," Addison replied baldly, watching whiskers move around.

"Bold words," the stranger chuckled nervously, both hands in the open on the table.

Addison had laid the Manticore off to one side where he could get at it quickly if he needed, but not an obvious threat.

Cowboy samurai who has just ridden into town. (Ridden? That was even weirder. He wanted to meet a horse, one of these days, as frightening as those monsters seemed to be.)

"Are you familiar with recent events on Gowook?" Addison smiled at the man.

"I am not," he shook his head. "Events locally have been such that they brought a Pyramid down on us to try to keep a lid on things."

"I do not fear a Pyramid," Addison said, leaning forward and putting his elbows on the table. "The time of the Innruld is almost over."

"Even bolder words," Briston replied. "What fills you with such confidence?"

"We have met a new alien species," Addison smiled. "Humans. Powerful. Dangerous. But currently friendly and willing to assist us in overthrowing the masters of the galaxy."

Addison had known Aileen long enough to read certain emotions that a Yithadreph could not fake. The way all the whiskers laid flat as though pulled back from behind, along with the ears. The way the eyes swelled and bulged. The little intake of breath.

"Truly?" Briston asked.

"At Gowook, although I was not there, they did enough damage that for several days, nobody was in control of orbital space, and a convoy of colony ships escaped," Addison continued. "They are currently en route to a planet in Human Space where they will be welcomed and resettled."

"What will happen at Oton Mari?" Briston asked quietly, also leaning forward now, his breath a little shallower than before.

"We would like to liberate it from Innruld control," Addison sat upright now and smiled.

Remarkably, Remahle hadn't said one stupid thing so far. Possibly a record for the man, who generally talked to hear his own voice rather than having anything to say.

Maybe Remahle was finally growing up? Wybert had, so *anything* was possible.

"Liberate?" Briston pressed.

"What would happen if all Innruld in-system were killed or driven off?" Addison asked. "If all their Security troopers with the long truncheons were eliminated? What would Oton Mari be like if the Innruld could not easily retake the station or the system?"

"How is that possible?" Briston snapped at him now. "They have Security Pyramids. Barcs. Guns and troops."

"And Oton Mari has been such a thorn in their sides that they have had to double down on control," Addison replied. "I propose to remove them entirely and let you decide your fate. After that, we will go after other systems and free them in turn."

"How would you kill all the Innruld?"

Addison smiled.

"Humans are six feet tall and weight two hundred pounds, at least the males," he said. "They can lift a one hundred pound weight completely over their head and throw a half pound weight a considerable distance with force and accuracy. And there are billions of them. Human Space has almost the populace on Innruld Space, but only a few aliens. Moah, Gnashiiley, and even Atomarsk."

"Atomarsk?!?"

"I have met them," Addison nodded. "Atomarsk H'Brige Slani is close enough now that we might take you to meet her sometime. The ship that escorted a convoy of Churquen and Yithadreph refugees was commanded by a Gnashiiley named Carlos Nguema. It is possible."

"Why would they help us?" Briston queried.

"They are part of a multi-species government called the Rio Alliance," Addison said. "Dedicated to a galaxy where all sentients are equally free. Personally, I would erase the Innruld completely, but others feel that we should just exile them when the time comes for the entire Species Underground to rise up. At least those that we allow to survive."

Addison watched the fellow come close to hyperventilating. He had the exact distance to his pistol in mind, in case this stranger turned out to be an Innruld agent, but he doubted that they would reveal themselves just yet. Especially with the bomb Addison had just dropped on them.

"How will they deal with a Pyramid?" Briston asked. "Nothing can resist such a beast."

Remahle laughed now. It was a quiet, contemplative chuckle just past a snort of derision.

"A three-day-old Galumph kit is about as dangerous to Lazarus as a Innruld Security Pyramid," Remahle said with such clinical detachment that Addison felt his own scales flare a little.

Briston Moora's ears went flat.

"Truly?" Briston wheezed.

"The discussion I heard was how many pieces they needed to carve that ship into when it came time," Remahle assured him calmly. "Not if they could win or even if the Innruld might somehow escape."

Addison hazarded a glance at Remahle but kept his jaw from falling open. Mostly.

Remahle smiled serenely and watched them back.

As near as Addison could remember, that outcome had not been a topic of conversation, and he couldn't see Aileen sharing such a tidbit with her assistant anyway. But for a lie Remahle had likely made from whole cloth, it made a frightful tale. All the more so because it was one hundred percent truth.

Carved up like dinner, already cooked and just lying on the table waiting.

Addison smiled and went along with it. Maybe Remahle really was growing up. Stranger things had happened.

"Now, you will need to brief your people," Addison said to the man, rising. "I will be at the same cafe tomorrow at roughly the same time as today to eat and perhaps discuss deals for resupply, if a broker were to come along."

Briston rose as well, still a little wide-eyed. He allowed himself to be seen to the airlock and politely sent on his way.

Once the airlock hatch closed fully, Remahle finally doubled over and giggled, sounding more like the cargo assistant Addison had known for so many years.

"That was priceless," he tittered between giggles.

"You had me going, Remahle," Addison admitted, which just caused him to break out in even greater giggles.

"Wait until Aileen hears," he finally managed, wiping away tears and randomly chortling. "Sorry. He was so tough and full of himself that I couldn't resist."

"Well, you certainly made an impact," Addison assured him.

"So what about tomorrow?" Remahle asked.

"Tomorrow, we have to live up to it."

SIXTEEN

AILEEN

SHE HAD STARTED with the ancient form of Tai Chi Chuan, and then moved on to other things. Aileen's first instructor had been Xiuying, who had been a bouncer after being a marine. Lucas was just a marine, and an officer, so he didn't have nearly as many rough edges as Xiuying. Nor had he killed anywhere as many people.

But the dojo mat was not a place for violence, except in intent. She moved slowly through the form, twisting and turning with her hips and spine and letting that throw hands and feet where they needed to be. Yithadreph weren't storks, like Humans. Didn't have impossibly long legs and arms to grab and kick. But she had a spine far more flexible, and that let her compete.

All Strav Ardna's people were in a Human hell, but the next time anyone came for her, Aileen would be prepared.

Lucas watched, waiting patiently as she finished the final set of forms. Xiuying had invented new things for her to do that took advantage of short stature, great flexibility, and the ability to climb when she needed. Part of what he had called Kung Fu, Aikido, and a few other bits and pieces he had picked up along the way. She hadn't taught Lucas yet, but supposed that she should at some point, just to get used to teaching others.

There were Yithadreph that would need to be able to knock an Innruld on his ass with these moves.

"Ready?" Lucas asked now.

Aileen nodded and he joined her. The form had many different names, but Xiuying had called it "push hands" even though that was something of a misnomer.

They touched the backs of their hands together and just let them press enough to keep contact. He began by pivoting on his hips, arm loose but held firmly in a way that drove his stork fingers at Aileen's face. She responded by rotating also on her hips, withdrawing her shoulders and using the twisting motion to move his hand past her head without touching.

It was Aileen's turn now and she let her hips shift forward, driving her shoulders towards him and striking out herself. Lucas blocked by similarly rotating his hips and drawing his arm to negate hers, neither of them pushing more than necessary to retain contact and read the intent of the other.

Stork boy had an unfair advantage in height and reach, being a foot and a half taller than her, but that just meant that she was used to dealing with Humans. Most of his kind would have no idea how to deal with an angry Yithadreph.

Similarly, he and Xiuying were probably the only two ready to fight against most of the Species, who tended to be shorter.

Well, all except Grace, but that woman could kill anything she encountered, so she didn't count.

They fell into rhythm. That was the key, making it so automatic that the body reacted without the mind needing to do anything at all.

After a while, they shifted to punching. Same technique as before. Lucas would slowly punch at her face with his right hand. She would block by touching the back of his hand as it closed, pushing it just enough off line to miss as her shoulders rotated. The return drove her fist at his face and he blocked using the same pattern. Back and forth. Slow kicks with the back foot were added to the punch, just to remind you to flex hard when punching and to keep the front foot off the ground.

Xiuying had been big on using his mass and speed to nail someone's foot to the deck when he got close to them, where his elbows and fists could get to work and you couldn't escape him. Aileen didn't have the mass to do that to a Human or Innruld, but he had introduced her to a hookstep that most people weren't prepared to evade. And when they did, the foot she owned would stay put just long enough to put a stork on his ass where she could get at his head quickly.

Aileen didn't like what Lazarus had turned her into, but all he had really done was introduce her to a new universe, bigger and scarier than the one she'd known before him. It had been Strav Ardna who taught her that a girl needed to be able to kill any bastard who got too close and wouldn't take no for an answer.

Xiuying and Lucas had just given her the vocabulary to express herself properly.

"You angry today?" Lucas asked.

Aileen realized that they had sped up to a speed where most people would have gotten hurt, but she was working with a trained killer and they had moved there gradually.

Good to know that she could.

Aileen hopped back instead of trying to explain or slowing down wrong and getting punched.

"Sorry," she said as they came to rest.

"Nobody is going to be able to do that to you again,

Aileen," he said seriously. "They'll have to go through me, Lazarus, and the rest first. And like before, I'll make sure they're all dead just for trying."

There. That was it. The Human penchant for violence. The Innruld didn't allow it, just like they didn't allow any sort of *dance* that might hide combat forms such as she had learned from these Humans.

"I'm okay," she decided. "Just keyed up. If something happens to Addison, you'll need me."

"If something happens to Addison, we'll be storming the gates of hell and making sure everyone over there goes through first," Lucas assured her with deadly certainty.

"Yes, but none of you fit in right now," she nodded, drawing a deep breath and deciding that she was done with close drills for now. "I'm the only one who can walk out of a shuttle and distract everyone long enough for your team to sneak aboard that station, or anyplace else. That's why I need to be ready to lead. Why Lazarus made me his Second Officer."

"You think it will come to that?" Lucas asked.

"I hope not," Aileen said. "But as you and Lazarus have reminded me more than once, the war has begun."

SEVENTEEN

CORMAC THE NAVCRAWLER

CORMAC HAD USED his infinite patience and singular focus to locate Ajax, hiding out there in the darkness of the Oton Mari system. Optical scans at maximum resolution had been necessary, but the Light Starcruiser was such an oddly unique shape that Cormac could take the time to wash out all the mere rocks and comets floating around.

It helped that Kuei had intended to park at a specific distance and simply listen. Lack of motion had been the key to finding them. Everything else moved in the star's gravitational field, either in the nearly-circular ellipse of a planetary disk orbit moving sideways, or the longer ellipticals of a mass disturbed by the near passage of a larger gravitational dimple to generate redshift/blurshift on motion.

Oton Mari had not developed many planets, as a close encounter with some other star early in its existence had caused proto-planets to be torn back asunder before they could properly coalesce. The result was a solar system filled with all manner of broken rock and ice that miners could explore, but only two planets that they could safely land on, with the one below him only marginally habitable and the other being hot enough for lead to melt on the surface.

Nobody could reply to anything Cormac sent, but he maintained a regular pattern of burst transmissions aimed at the spot where Ajax waited. Lazarus would appreciate at least this half of a conversation, and Addison had written up his meeting with the local underground group.

Cormac paused everything and emitted what would appear to other vessels in the vicinity as a navigational ping. Like perhaps the NavCrawler aboard the ship was one of his less-intelligent relatives and didn't know that he could stop doing that when docked. Or maybe was too paranoid about navigational hazards.

Cormac didn't have the highest opinion of some of his cousins.

But it gave him cover to pulse nearby space, perhaps a little harder than was necessary, and watching with sensors that had been radically upgraded with equipment from Dutra's stores to the point that Cormac suspected Ajax was the only ship with better eyes in the system.

He maintained a detailed map of every ship in nearby space: coming, going, or parked. All that got transmitted regularly to Ajax and Kuei, just in case. The Security Pyramid was parked in an orbit that was optimal for the wall of weapons on this facing to engage anything that had undocked and presented a threat, but Cormac had access to a Star Spear if he really needed it. He had reviewed the logs of Wybert's various engagements on Gowook, so he was prepared for violence, if such became necessary.

NavCrawlers were not supposed to be revolutionaries, either, but he'd been reprogrammed a few times, and also left to his own devices for decades at a time. Plus, he had met the Human known as Lazarus of Bethany. Read the ancient Human book detailing why the Human Pancho *thought that to be a proper name to assume.*

Cormac could do the same. He just hadn't picked a name yet.

So he sat and quietly watched nearby space for any hint of trouble.

EIGHTEEN

ADDISON

ADDISON DIDN'T MIND RETURNING to this restaurant. The food yesterday had been pretty good. Comfort food, nothing grand or extravagant, but *Ajax* had no Galumph strips in the larder.

Sometimes, a man had a hankering.

They were at the same table as yesterday. The bar keeper was the same Zentra, perhaps a little less formal today. Perhaps not. The crowd was of the same size, but Addison could not readily tell if they were the same players as yesterday, or just the same roles.

And he ordered the Galumph strips again, with oil-fried vegetables on the side. Lazarus had spoiled him with Belgian Fries in salt.

Remahle had accompanied him as well, dressed like a dock worker, which was close enough to his usual duty. Without Aileen, he was in charge of cargo and supplies, although Addison fully intended to go over all the paperwork twice before it got transmitted. He had money to buy things, but still had a niggling doubt about whether Remahle was up to it.

However, maybe the Kr'mari had finally grown up. If so, now was when everyone should find out. Especially as Admiral da Silva was intending to build a fleet of captured and impressed Innruld vessels as a start.

Building Star Spears and Star Lances was far easier than building a warship from scratch, not that anything could stand against a Westphalian GunWall, or even a ScoutWall.

But it would free the Churquen and the Yithadreph from the Innruld. That was the first step.

They were just about done with their lunch when a figure entered and caught Addison's eye.

Another Yithadreph male. Older, in that his fur was starting to turn white around the edges of his face. Shorter than Briston or even Aileen. Pudgy in the manner of someone who doesn't swim enough and eats rich food.

Exceptionally well dressed, as well. Tan jumpsuit with dark brown swirls worked into the fabric.

The stranger smiled and ambled slowly this way, stopping close enough to talk normally without intruding.

"May I help you?" Addison asked politely, stuffing the last bit of meat in his mouth and chewing quickly.

"You are the director of *Star of Kilri?*" the man asked in a voice with no doubt whatsoever.

"I am."

"Remy Hendams," he introduced himself with a half-bow. "Ships Chandlery and Resupply. A little bird whispered in my ear that you might be here today to talk about resupplying your vessel for where you might go next, after seeing the extraordinary sights at Oton Mari, such as they are."

"Join us," Addison gestured to the empty chair and watched the man sit and then telescope it up to a comfortable level to talk. He leaned close enough to talk without being overheard. "Expansion."

"Equal."

"Surprise."

"Watch."

"Pledge."

"Registration," Remy completed the cycle quietly. "It is a pleasure to meet you, Addison Wolcott and Remahle Mebarsu. Briston had interesting things to say, although I am not sure I believe them."

Addison shrugged. He might not have believed such a thing from a total stranger, either. But then he smiled, because they were all true.

"I merely need to know how to assist," Addison said simply. "Discounting the Pyramid, how many Innruld and troopers are there on station?"

"Discounting?" Remy asked, a little put out, perhaps. "Only a handful of Innruld themselves, as the masters dislike serving in this system, but must because so much mineral trade goes on. Troopers number several hundred, counting anyone that might carry a weapon."

"And what would the locals do if someone started capturing or eliminating them?" Addison asked.

"Briston mentioned your allies," Remy nodded. "Are they that dangerous?"

"They can be, but we did not bring enough of them with us to simply overwhelm the local security apparatus," Addison replied. "However, I do have experts at violence. How would you neutralize this station? I am more familiar with the standard Skycity design than this organic mess."

Remy smiled now and leaned forward. Addison noted that the keeper had not come over to ask about refills or the needs of the newcomer, but then he was hopefully part of the organization, or at least sympathetic.

"They are less centralized," Remy said with a gleam in his eyes. "Each lobe of the station has a security office, and an

Innruld officer in charge, because they need to be in so many different places at once."

"So we might take each one individually?" Addison inquired, wondering a little as he did that he might also be turning into what the Humans called a General as well. "Would the locals be able to distract the rest as we did?"

"Perhaps, but again, we must ask why," Remy said.

"Because my allies would like to help the Species Underground liberate everyone else in Innruld Space from the masters of the galaxy," Addison said. "Simple as that. My mate is currently leading a convoy of vessels into the Human sectors to establish a colony safe from Innruld interference. Is that enough?"

"And the Pyramid?" Remy asked, as if that might be the surprise that disrupted everyone's plans.

"We might destroy it," Addison said negligently. "Or allow them to barely escape with their lives. It depends on how the locals respond. There was always the possibility that you folks had become accustomed to the chains around your necks and were perhaps loathe to remove them."

It was a low blow, but Addison really didn't have decades to convince people to rise up. The Innruld needed to be beaten now, before Westphalia could somehow invade this side of the nebula and change all the equations.

Remy's face soured in a way that wasn't immediately obvious unless you'd known Yithadreph for as long as Addison had.

"What do you propose?" Remy asked.

"Sneaking a force onto this station and using it to permanently, materially damage the security forces handy," Addison said. "Letting the local merchants and miners practice self-government for a while as we go off and hunt Innruld in other places."

"Can you do it?" Remy gasped.

Addison glanced around, but only the keeper was paying attention now, so he leaned in.

"Yes," he stated flatly. "Can you gather your forces? If so, I will go get the people I need and return shortly to put things in motion."

"We must meet these Humans," Remy said, turning serious and cold now.

"Who will you send that you trust?" Addison smiled.

"Briston Moora would be a good candidate, if you approve," the man leaned back now. "He has been with the organization for a long time and we can rely on his judgment."

"Excellent," Addison said. "Would you also be able to provide us with some supplies, such that perhaps Briston is part of the group that delivers them and accidentally gets left behind?"

"That would work," Remy said. He reached into a pocket and pulled out a card, handing it to Addison. "Send your messages here and I will get you quotes for things."

He rose with a nod to both of them and withdrew with the dignity of the aged.

Addison turned to Remahle and noted the careful smile in the man's eyes.

"Thoughts?"

"All things represent some level of risk," the Kr'mari said cogently. "This perhaps less than others, unless we've blundered into a huge Innruld trap and they are going to try to capture *Star of Kilri*."

"How would you handle that, cargo master?" Addison asked.

"Oh, I'll open and inspect every box that comes aboard for bombs, stowaways, or anything else," Remahle turned as serious as Aileen now, but that wasn't the worst role model. "We'll only take the one kid, and he'll be unarmed and locked in a cabin while we go meet Lazarus. I presume a short-hop outside this system to meet up and move strike teams around before we return?"

"Something like that," Addison agreed. "You ready for your part?"

"You did say yesterday that we were going to have to live up to our legend."

NINETEEN

LAZARUS

LAZARUS READ THE REPORT AGAIN, unsure but willing to trust Addison's judgment on these things. He was in his day office, with Rod seated across from him, also reading on a tablet.

The man looked up now.

"Thoughts?" Rod asked.

"You'll get your chance to have the Pyramid or the station shoot first," Lazarus said, only half joking. "Nothing we've seen suggests that *Ajax*'s forward shielding is at risk from anything in the system. Hell, Addison's Star Spear is more powerful than anything on the Pyramid."

"Noted," Rod grimaced. "It's the part about launching a commando raid that had me concerned."

"With your permission, sir, I'd like to accompany it, or possibly lead it," Lazarus said.

"You are the Captain of this boat, Lazarus," Rod growled.

"And the only person here who has ever engaged in close combat with anyone from this region," Lazarus reminded him. "Aileen has some training, but has never thrown a punch in anger. The time on Yisan she was fighting for her life. Lucas is good, but still a rookie. At his age, I was doing things you might not be allowed to know about."

"Oh, Pedro Santos told me about some of it when he sent me out to find you," Rod laughed. "I might remind you that you aren't twenty anymore. Why you? Who will remain in command here, if we have you, Addison, and Aileen all on the station?"

"I believe you have commanded a warship in Rio service," Lazarus grinned. "Presumably you haven't forgotten *everything* you know."

"Very funny," Rod smiled.

"Seriously, Rod," Lazarus continued. "Wybert and Kuei both know what they are doing, and are combat veterans aboard *Ajax*. You just need to issue directions and let them handle it. Just don't blow up the station while I'm over there, please?"

"Can you do it, *Pancho*?" he asked now.

"Innruld control is fear-based, Rod," Lazarus replied. "People are afraid to speak up. But the miners are so rowdy normally that they don't like the crackdown. If we break that, the Innruld would have to work four or five times as hard to regain it. Meanwhile, others will see that it can be done."

Rod was silent for a while. Lazarus watched. The admiral could still overrule him and order Lazarus not to join the assault force. Not that da Silva would replace him. At least Lazarus didn't think so.

"What is a greater impact to the Innruld?" Rod finally asked. "Annihilating the Pyramid entirely, or damaging it so badly that they have to scrap it?"

"We're going to have a lot of prisoners if this works," Lazarus replied. "Not all of them are evil bastards or thugs. Some just wanted a job. Others probably saw it as a way out of the lower classes, where their kids might have an edge to a better education and jobs with the state. I don't intend to kill everyone we can lay hands on, so we'll be sending the lot home on private vessels. A dead Pyramid in orbit probably says more than anything, but I'll let you make that call when the time comes. Nothing says you have to melt the damned thing down into unrecognizable scrap. In fact, I think you can permanently immobilize it with two shots, one through the control space at the tip and one through the engineering controls at the bottom."

"Then they surrender?" Rod asked.

"Then you can give them the option, at least," Lazarus nodded. "I can't sit here and honestly tell you that they won't choose that hill to die on, Rod. But this is a war, and there will be casualties."

"Then I would appreciate it if you shut that station down hard and fast when the time comes," Rod finally smiled. "So I don't have to compete with Addison for body count. Neither of us are close to you, and I'd rather keep it that way."

Lazarus smiled.

"Thank you, Rod."

"Oh, you'll earn it," he replied. "Of that I have no doubt."

Lazarus didn't think he could disagree.

TWENTY

GRACE

GRACE FOUND it amusing that as tough a man as he was, not even Lazarus was willing to just give her orders and expect her to jump. Except maybe when he ordered her to bed because he wanted to fool around some.

And even then, there was always a smile involved.

So they had fooled around. Possibly even dozed a little after a particularly hard orgasm, which was kind of what she had needed anyway.

Grace was upright, with her back against a pile of pillows, while Lazarus was leaned against her shoulder and more or less draped across her.

She liked the feel of skin, even as strange as the contrast was between her dark brown and his paleness with freckles.

"So I have a request," he finally began, although she had been waiting for some time.

"Yes?" Grace leaned down and kissed the top of his head where things were starting to come in more gray than orange now.

"I have Rod's approval to lead the assault on the station," he continued, tracing one hand absently up her far hip where the nerves were warm and sensitive. "Aileen will be our scout because she can fit in with the locals. I was hoping I might convince you to join us in your official, militant capacity."

"You need a ninja?" she teased.

"I don't know who yet, but someone will need to be made an example of," Lazarus said, turning now enough that he was looking up at her instead of at her breast. "You are the best one here to just take someone down, without necessarily killing them. I'm not sure Aileen could kill someone except by accident. My reflexes might be to destroy someone we wanted to keep alive, because when I was much younger, we didn't need prisoners."

"And I might need to make that decision in a split second?" Grace asked.

"I don't know anybody better trained or more skilled on the topic, anywhere in the Rio Alliance Navy."

And he was probably right. They trained for close combat, but that was just an adjunct. They also trained in damage control and firefighting, ship's maintenance and all the other things that came with being a sailor.

Only she spent several hours every day working on movement and strength. Muscle memory. Automatic reflexes to kill or stun. And she was certainly qualified with a much wider range of weapons, although she doubted that the greatbow would be necessary for this mission. A long knife like a wakizashi would probably be sufficient, in addition to a stun pistol, although with so many species to engage, one could never be sure if it would stun, kill, or do nothing. A greatsword like her Daichi would probably frighten a few people to death by itself.

"Please?" he asked, mistaking her tactical planning for second thoughts.

Grace would have never followed this man this far if she hadn't grown convinced that what he was doing was right, even when he wasn't always sure. Nobody else ever saw those doubts, but she was there in the middle of the night when he might rouse from a nightmare but never come fully conscious.

She had heard the words, the fears, the dreams.

"Of course," she said, kissing him again, just because she could.

Very few people she had ever met had impressed Grace Savidge with their drive and willingness to lay it all on the line for their beliefs.

"Thank you," he said with immense conviction.

Nothing more, but nothing more was needed, as he had packed it all into those two words. His trust, even his love.

She could conquer Innruld Space for him, because he believed in her.

TWENTY-ONE

AILEEN

AILEEN LOOKED at all the damned storks that she would be leading into battle. Guiding maybe. Something.

The staging bay on *Ajax* was huge, even with a combat team ready to board *Kilri* for the run back to Oton Mari. Most of them were too damned serious, but Lazarus and Grace were smiling. Lucas had gone so sourpuss that she wanted to tickle the man, just to break things up.

She turned to Addison instead. He was smiling. Mostly. There was more fear there, but he'd never even imagined doing something this insane. He had been elsewhere when she went to Yisan with Eha and Lazarus. And there met Grace and the others who were now all back in Rio space protecting her stubby tail from those weirdos.

The strange kid was standing on the far side of Addison, like he was more afraid of her than he was the Humans in dark-gray tactical gear with enough firepower to invade a planet, casually hooked or in pockets.

"Briston, you with me?" she asked, maybe with a little more snap in her voice than was absolutely necessary.

His eyes centered on her and shifted some. Drifted some, down to inspect her.

Shit. She was used to Lazarus doing that, but she usually ignored the other males who tended to notice she was a woman.

She cocked a hip and put a fist on it. Those eyes snapped right back up to hers.

"Good," she said. "Now, we're going to bounce back through trans-space to the station, where Addison here will tell them we had a breakdown of some sort and needed to limp back so we could fix it. Clear so far?"

"Yes, ma'am," Briston said.

They'd been over this all once with the kid, but he'd been in shock meeting Humans at the time. The storks did that to people, being so damned tall and with shoulders wide enough to rockclimb.

And guns. Lots of guns.

Hopefully, everyone here was at least half as good as Xiuying had been, so nobody would singe her tail accidentally. Aileen had no doubt that she would be out front, walking with this goofball Yithadreph kid like they were on a hot date or something.

He was cute, but not *that* cute. But it would deflect folks.

"You know where all the security stations are, right?" Aileen pointed her jaw and whiskers at him, just so he stopped looking at her chest.

Kid snapped to again.

"Yes, Aileen," he said, drawing himself up to his full four foot ten. Almost came to attention like a sailor, but he didn't know that.

"Good, because we won't know where they will put us, so we'll just have to hit the closest one and hold it," she said. "This ship will be along, but they'll probably be busy killing the Pyramid so they can't help us. You are on your own with the rest of us, so your job will be to send out the call for the rest of the Species Underground to start getting restless. And I want more than just a bar fight. Am I clear?"

He gulped and nodded.

Aileen turned back to Lazarus and watched the grin disappear from his face, but not fast enough that she missed it.

"I guess we're ready," she informed him. "Admiral da Silva, you listening?"

"Affirmative, Commander," the Human boss answered immediately. "Good luck on your end and we'll be along."

She grumbled, but there was nothing to it. Grace and Lazarus had done this, with Xiuying and Oluchi, back on Yisan, after that bastard Ardna had sent his goons with fists and shock rods.

Still, it had taken four of them that night, and that was before she knew anything about Human fighting.

"All hands, deploy to *Star of Kilri*," Aileen ordered, reaching out to give Addison a quick squeeze as she went by and turning Briston the right direction.

He boarded ahead of her, and the entire Bolivian Army followed behind.

She'd actually had to make Lazarus dig up that ancient video, once he used the term in casual conversation, just so she understood what it meant.

The two bank robbers hadn't gotten away. Got killed for their effort. So she wanted to make sure what it meant that the whole Bolivian Army was on her side. Following.

And they were.

Into the old dump of a wreck, sitting at tables in the wardroom, which was really the only place to hold a dozen combat storks and all their firepower. She ended up next to Briston, but wasn't surprised. She was the only non-Human in the room, with everyone else on the bridge or back in engineering. Even Khyaa'sha was absent, probably holding something perfectly still while Thadrakho welded it.

In better repair didn't mean fixed. Just meant fewer things breaking down. Aileen already missed *Ajax*.

Outside, the airlocks broke their kiss and went the way of former lovers on a train platform, as *Star of Kilri* turned and prepared to jump back to Oton Mari. Ten-minute hop and they would be back, all set to commit armed mayhem.

Aileen kept her grumbles mostly to herself.

"Are they really enough to capture the whole station?" Briston whispered, voice up a half octave like hers had been when she'd first seen the Human across from her stripped nude as his suit came off.

Muscles. Height. Mass. Violence.

"They are," she replied.

The damned galaxy probably wasn't safe if they hadn't turned out to be like Rio.

Westphalia, for example. Specist, on top of everything else.

The Innruld had, according to ancient legend, bred themselves for pure beauty, with the modern example usually seven-plus feet tall, but only two hundred to two twenty pounds. Long, elegant limbs and fingers. Drawn, aquiline faces. Long, fine hair, usually white or perhaps blond.

Looking around, she understood why Lazarus called himself an orc, but she'd had to watch those ancient vids to understand the reference, where Innruld were supposedly the pretty elves. Humans were special. Shorter, broader, tougher, stronger that the Innruld.

Meaner, too, but that was a factor of her being around military volunteers. The Innruld were just petty aristocrats with a social structure geared to support their every desire.

It wasn't like she hadn't spent half a decade smuggling the sorts of narcotics specifically designed to ruin Innruld lives.

Get them stoned enough and they stopped caring about things. Stopped breeding. Stopped doing.

Stopped.

Couple more of them were going to stop, when Aileen and her friends arrived for the party. But they'd brought it on themselves in a number of ways. Gowook was just the most recent case.

She turned her attention back to Briston, watched him flinch back from staring at her. She took a deep breath rather than lash him with the sharp edge of her tongue.

He was just a kid, even though he wasn't much younger than her. Seen far less of the galaxy. Done fewer stupid things. But he was in the Underground. They had to keep their noses clean at all times.

"What?" she asked, hopefully in a nicer tone than she might have.

"What will you do after you capture Oton Mari?" he asked, apparently screwing up the courage.

She glanced over at Lazarus, but he wasn't going to help. This was a Species issue. He was just the muscle along to wedge open a sticky door for her.

"We're going to be free," she said. "That probably means we find a bunch of miners we can recruit and capture some ships that we can turn into proper pirates, instead of just smuggling. Then we go break the Innruld."

Shit, now she sounded like Addison on one of his bad days. But then, she was Second Officer, right behind him in line of command, over on *Ajax*.

Kid got nervous.

"Recruiting?" he asked quietly.

"Yeah," she nodded. "*Ajax* is undercrewed for a lot of reasons, but we're reconfiguring things for non-Humans. Plus, Human technology is way better, so we're a social revolution as well as a military one. Why?"

"I might want to volunteer, sir," he said, lips pursed and whiskers and ears out straight sideways.

Not fearful, but nervous. Like maybe he was asking her out on a date.

Hell of a first date, even for a kid as cute as him. She smiled.

"Let's see how you do under fire, sailor," she replied.

Lazarus made a snorting noise under his breath that told her he was listening to everything, but hadn't stepped in to speak, so he was leaving it up to her. Or was he match-making? She didn't get to have him scrub her back nearly as much as in the old days, now that Grace was around. Although Grace's fingers had better nails on them, come to think of it.

She grinned at Lazarus and wondered if Briston would be utterly embarrassed to wash her back.

Hell of a bar to clear, but she'd known a few people bold enough.

"All hands, stand by for trans-space," Addison's voice came over the line.

Aileen smiled at the kid.

Shit was about to get interesting.

TWENTY-TWO

ADDISON

BACK TO OTON MARI. Gone for all of about four hours. Addison sighed and focused on sounding aggrieved rather than nervous.

"Open a channel to the station," he ordered Cormac as they dropped out of trans-space.

Nothing had changed.

"*Star of Kilri*, what is your status?" a gruff male voice came through the speakers.

"We suffered a life support rupture in trans-space," Addison replied. "Dropped out and turned around so we could dock at the station and draw air if the whole system failed while we were fixing it."

Shiva Zephyr Glaive used to do that about once a year. Except where he usually was, everyone had to get into their suits while Thadrakho and Ereshkiki Nisab tore everything apart and fixed it. Only once had it gotten bad enough that Addison had gotten worried.

And this ship was still in far better shape that *Shiva Zephyr Glaive*.

Long pause on the comm as they thought about it. At

least they didn't have the sorts of sensors that would let them identify the dozen Humans currently aft. They might just open fire on him at that point, if they had any sense.

The Pyramid hadn't moved in the intervening period. Still parked over there making people nervous just by standing off to one side like a grownup supervising rowdy teens. *Star of Kilri* wasn't going to pass too close, but they were all on the same side of the station itself.

"*Star of Kilri*, you will dock with the Security Pyramid for inspection," the order came suddenly.

Addison kept his curses to himself. Now was not the time to give them any reason to suspect anything. Probably already thought he was a smuggler or something, to have returned so quickly.

Or they were bored and wanted to harass someone, and Addison had happened to drop into their line of sight at the wrong minute.

"Understood, Security," he said. Not much he could say. They outgunned him by orders of magnitude, even with the Star Spear in the main turret. "Please provide a vector and dock location."

"Transmitting," the man on the Pyramid said. "Follow this course exactly or you will be destroyed."

Addison cut the line and sighed again.

"Cormac, fly exactly like they want us to," he said.

"*Course engaged, Addison*," Cormac replied. "*What will we do next?*"

"This is where things maybe get a little complicated."

TWENTY-THREE

LAZARUS

LAZARUS HEARD the sound of Addison's keel scales as he approached the wardroom, so he already knew something was wrong. He reached out and just touched Grace's hand, but she had apparently identified the sound as well.

"Quiet," Lazarus said in a voice loud enough to invoke it.

Addison appeared, scales a little gray, for lack of a better description.

"We have a problem," Addison began. "We have returned to Oton Mari, but the Security Pyramid ordered us to dock there for inspection."

"Suppose they realize where we stole the ship from in the first place?" Aileen asked.

"It is possible," Addison nodded.

After all, it had been a small Security Barc at one point. Lazarus's people had torn it apart, cleaned it up, and modified the external lines with various things to disguise it, but someone might have recognized the underlying hull.

"What do we do now?" Addison asked.

"Make sure that Cormac keeps the transponder turned up loud, so that *Ajax* realizes where we are when they drop out of jump on top of the beast," Lazarus said. "I don't want Kirov hitting a section of the Pyramid where we are while we're busy capturing it."

"You what?" Addison blinked several times and all of his visible scales flared away from his skin, almost to the tip of his tail.

"Imagine how much more fun piracy will be if we started with a Pyramid and upgunned it, Addison," Lazarus smiled.

The look on that Churquen's face was priceless. Lazarus was sorry he didn't have a camera recording it.

"Capture a Pyramid?" he wheezed.

"We were going to capture an entire station," Lazarus reminded him. "I suspect that this will be even easier, as there is likely to only be one control space we'll need to eliminate or take."

"Wasn't *Ajax* set to kill the ship when it arrived?" Addison offered.

"You'll need to tell Wybert not to kill another ship I'm flying on, okay?" Lazarus smiled.

That got through to the man. He and Aileen both snickered after a moment of raw shock.

"Besides, there are other Security Barcs around here that Wybert can destroy to make a point," Lazarus continued.

"Are you people insane?" Briston Moora spoke up now, still sitting across from Lazarus with his head going back and forth like a ping pong match.

"They are," Aileen spoke up before Lazarus could say anything. "Completely, unreservedly, illogically insane. And they can do it. Don't forget that part. Before, you and I were going to move along ahead of them, distracting and deflecting people while we got the Humans where they needed to go. Now we have to run like hell, because they move too fast for anyone else to keep up."

"It won't be a dead run, like it was at Zhoonarrim,"

Lazarus told her. "I suspect it will be a running series of gun battles, with them bringing pain sticks and maybe stun pistols until they finally get smart and open the armory for heavy firepower."

"Will a stunner not work on Humans?" Briston gasped now.

"Not well," Grace smiled at the kid. "Most of us will also have armor that insulates them to a certain extent."

"But there are ten thousand beings on that ship…" Briston tried a new tack.

"And we need to make sure that most of them are too busy doing other things to concentrate on us," Lazarus said. He turned to Addison with a grim smile. "You will need to open fire with the Star Spear once we're clear. And maybe abandon this ship and move into the station in case they figure out how to fire back."

Everyone fell deathly silent, but most of the Humans were gunners and engineers, not boarding marines like he and Lucas. It would have been nice to have Xiuying handy.

"This ship is a tool," Lazarus reminded them. "Use it up if you have to, but make sure you don't get yourself killed in the process, okay?"

"*Lazarus, what would happen if we fired into the control center from the outside while this ship is docked?*" Cormac's voice came over the intercom now. "*There are secondary control spaces, but we are likely to have eliminated most if not all of the senior Innruld officers if we were to do such a thing.*"

Lazarus marveled. He'd always been nervous about the Crawlers. Silicon intelligence rather than organic. Back home, they had proven to be too inflexible to handle the sorts of things Humans took for granted, as they still had to follow a decision tree that was only as good as the programmers who set it up.

As Cormac liked to remind him occasionally, the being

had over a century of uptime, and had proven himself a valuable member of the crew more than once.

But they weren't supposed to kill people. That was programmed in on day one, so that they didn't decide to wipe out the organics and just rule the ruins as electronic life forms. At least that was the end point of the logic.

"If you have that shot and take it, Cormac, you are likely to seriously undermine the ability of the Pyramid to resist infection by Humans," Lazarus replied. "And they will try to destroy you, so it will likely be critical to abandon ship as soon as you do something like that."

Addison nodded.

"I guess we'll be right behind you," he said. "Let me prep the others. We'll be docking in about five minutes."

Lazarus looked around. The two Yithadreph had shifted to panic and not returned yet. Lucas was smiling. Grace was calm. The others were nervous, but phlegmatic.

Nobody ever promised a sailor that they would die in bed, after all.

TWENTY-FOUR

LAZARUS

LAZARUS HAD everyone except Grace back in the wardroom while Addison stood near the airlock door. Around them, the ship clunked heavily as the docking arm took hold and pulled the ship over to the airlock where it would be secure.

Somebody wasn't taking chances, as a second arm caught the ship forward with a different thump, and a third aft secured the engines. There would not be any escape for the ship, until someone took over the controls inside and released things.

But then, the Security forces on the other side of the lock were expecting to be dealing with smugglers. Not Human assault troops.

With any luck, he could go through them like shit through a goose, leaving a trail of bodies out cold, or maybe dead, depending. They had always expected that *Ajax* was going to shatter this vessel when it arrived, so casualties were likely to be heavy.

And all of these people were Security Police, rather than merchants, miners, or homemakers, so they could not claim that they had white hands. Especially not with the things the Innruld had them do to others.

It was an old argument. Some level of state force was necessary to protect the nation and enforce the laws. But when the authorities stopped answering to the people, you started down the road to aristocracy, where an inherited minority had all the rights and the majority existed to serve.

In the case of Innruld Space, throw in the distinction of being born Innruld to put you in the elite and everyone else second or third class at best. Lock things down for the Churquen or Yithadreph. Limit their economies and education until they were all struggling just to survive.

Lazarus had heard the stories from Aileen about the building on Gowook where he had rescued her. The ancient flooring and dirty walls. The despair and crippling paranoia.

An interstellar civilization did not need a secret police. They needed an explorer corps, a colonization force, and enough beat cops to keep graffiti to a minimum.

Of course, if the economy was growing and vibrant, you didn't have nearly as much time to commit crime, because most people could get rich at legitimate jobs.

The Innruld would not allow that. Lazarus had a point to make. They would start with this Security Pyramid rather than Oton Mari Station, but the end result would still be revolution, as *Ajax* could not be denied.

"Lazarus, out main turret has the ability to deploy and engage," Cormac said quietly over the intercom. *"It appears that two turrets on the Pyramid might be a threat to this ship. I will endeavor to destroy those as well."*

"Thank you, Cormac," he said. "Then the rest of you get clear so you are safe."

"Understood."

"Are you ready, my friend?" Lazarus turned to Addison.

"I have dreamed about striking such a blow for decades,

Lazarus," Addison replied. "But I never imagined that it would actually occur."

Lazarus nodded.

"Just get them aboard and we'll take it from there," he said.

He nodded to Grace and the two of them took up opposite sides of the airlock door, in the hallway that ran the length of the ship. She was unarmed. He had an Ares tuned down from a tight, killing beam into something more like a flashlight with the kick of a small mule. Might still kill, but more likely to knock someone on their ass hard enough to leave them out cold.

At least long enough. The team had brought a stupid number of plastic ties to bind wrists and ankles, and most species were not strong enough nor flexible enough to escape such things. Nor did they have the history of violence and resistance that was common on Human worlds.

Lazarus reminded himself that he was making the galaxy a better place by giving the largest number of people the freedom to define their own success and pursue it.

*…vida, liberdade e a busca pela
felicidade…*

Addison slithered into the airlock and waited for the banging on the outside indicating a safe environment. Lazarus heard the door beep as it opened inward and took a deep breath.

"You are the director of this vessel?" an angry voice sounded up the hallway.

"I am," Addison replied calmly.

"What failure caused you to return?"

"Primary coolant pump suffered some sort of short," Addison said. "We're running on the backup, but may need to tear the whole system apart to fix it. We did last time, and it was just as easy to return here as to land on Tatau."

"You will show us," the man ordered.

"As you wish," Addison said.

Lazarus heard Addison pivoting in place on his keel scales and heading back up the airlock. Grace was aft, so he signaled her to drift back a little ways. She nodded and moved on utterly silent feet while Lazarus sat poised.

Addison appeared and curled around the long corner with that turning grace that only a snake could achieve, like a green sidewinder on hot sand, touching corners where the walls met the deck to push off.

An Innruld officer appeared next. The height of his shadow was enough to identify him. Lazarus watched as the man turned the corner as well, expecting the requisite two troopers that would accompany him everywhere.

The first was a Necherle, just like Thadrakho but not as tall. Just as gangling. Not a serious risk in close combat with he or Grace.

The other was a Kreeghal. Greco-Roman wrestlers by design, they were four feet tall but had arms as long as a Human, nearly dragging on the floor. Short, stubby legs that didn't let them move quickly, but arms and shoulders like a Human weightlifter. The only thing they didn't have was a good rotatrr cuff that would let them throw a rock or swing a sword overhand.

Still exceptionally dangerous.

"What is this?" the Innruld demanded.

Lazarus shot the Kreeghal square in the back from close enough that the bolt drove him into the Necherle. Both went down, and Lazarus shot the pile of bodies again, just because he had no interest in finding out who would win on the matt today.

When he looked up, Addison had turned and was

holding a pistol on the Innruld. Grace seemed to emerged from the bulkhead itself and took the man's hand in hers, spinning him around and popping the back of his knee to bring him down to her level.

"Shut up, or I will begin breaking things," Grace whispered lovingly into the man's ears as she bound his wrists. "You will answer my questions and do so quietly, or I will put you out the aft airlock nude by opening the door very slowly. Am I clearly understood?"

A pistol and a handcomm got liberated, but he was not resisting right now.

Lazarus peeked around the corner to look out of the airlock, rather than watching what was going on with the Innruld. Nobody was in sight, but that just meant that the man hadn't brought more troops with him.

"How many engineers on the dock just outside my ship?" Addison asked.

Somebody didn't want to answer, so got poked, eliciting a pained gasp.

"Four," the man whispered hoarsely. "You'll never get away with this."

"If I were you, I'd worry more about surviving the next five minutes," Addison informed the man. "Let us worry about whether or not we can capture or destroy your entire vessel. Who else is on the dock?"

"Nobody!" he gasped and Lazarus saw where Grace had tugged on an ear. Not bad, just attention-getting.

"Hopefully, you are correct," Grace said.

Lazarus knew how strong she was, in spite of being so lean. She dragged the man into the first chamber, already set up for such a thing. Lazarus kept watch while the Kreeghal and the Necherle also got disarmed and moved into storage. Grace locked the door from the outside and smiled at him.

Lazarus stuck his head in the wardroom now.

"Aileen, I need you to just walk right out the hatch like you know where you are going," he told her. "Distract the four people there long enough for the rest of us to take them down. Questions?"

"Just me, or both of us Yithadreph?"

"Briston, you up for some misdirection?" he turned to the other.

"I think so," the fellow said with a gulp.

"Just walk out there with me," Aileen told him. "You'll do fine, because we'll confuse them. Humans would set off all sorts of alarms in their heads."

"Okay."

"Go," Lazarus gestured the two of them.

Aileen had a stunner in one hand, concealed. Briston's was tucked in a pocket for now, but that was fine. Lazarus would have both of them in sight and all his troops poised to rush forward that point.

They moved. He watched.

Rather than just walk randomly, Aileen moved to the center of the space he could see and stopped.

It looked like a large bay, well-lit with white walls but scuffed and dirty like a landing bay should be. Lazarus couldn't see anybody else, but Aileen turned to her left.

Behind him, he felt Grace summon the others, a low rumbling of a dozen people moving as quietly as possible.

"Hey, which of you folk is in charge?" Aileen yelled at the room. "The officer told me to grab a couple of engineers to help my people with the life support system tear down."

"What's going on?" somebody out of sight on the left answered. Might have been female, but hard to tell.

Aileen shrugged theatrically and pointed with the hand not holding the stunner.

"He said to bring some folks to help out," she replied. "I just do cargo."

"Fine," that same someone said with an exasperated sigh.

Lazarus heard boots on the deck plate and figured that he had everyone looking the right way, so he moved. Grace would cover the right as he was going left. Lucas would cover the center. The others were there to handle firefights as they might occur.

Lazarus stepped out and shot another Yithadreph right in the center of her body, knocking her into an Aknaan that had been following. He shot that creature as well and looked around.

Aileen was firing at a pair standing around surprised. The Zentra and the Kdari went down hard, dropping their rifles as they collapsed.

"More prisoners," Lazarus gestured. "Wrap them up for now and we'll move them to the pyramid later if we can."

Bodies swarmed past him and started grabbing aliens while Lazarus moved to the far side of the dock. Aileen dragged Briston with her to the console and began working controls.

Quickly, they owned the space and were prepared to move inward.

First stage was complete.

Now, things would get dicey.

TWENTY-FIVE
AILEEN

AILEEN STUDIED the console in front of her. She had no idea what passwords were needed, but the woman working here hadn't locked anything when she walked off, so Aileen had complete control for the moment. One quick glance to make sure that everything was quiet and she nodded to Lazarus.

"Get Addison," she called to Lucas. "He can monitor things from here."

Anyone wandering along would be surprised, but there were no bodies lying around or making noise, so he could pretend to be a goon until he needed to shoot someone. Hopefully, everyone else would be too busy dealing with an invasion to worry about *Kilri* anyway.

Quickly, she called up a map of the station and studied the path and destination like another one of her cargo puzzles. Fewest steps. Least movement. Greatest density.

Nobody did it better than she did.

Lazarus was watching the door when Aileen had an idea.

"Lazarus," she called, causing him to turn. "Get me the uniform off the Yithadreph woman you shot and I can impersonate her. Briston can be my prisoner and we'll go right back to the con game where I'm on point."

She saw him hesitate, but then he nodded and sent one of the gunners off. She'd have done it the other way around, but the woman's uniform was cut for breasts and would look weird on a male.

And she needed to be in charge. Briston was nice, but he wasn't ready for armed mayhem with the storks.

Aileen stripped as someone brought her a new tunic. Briston's whisker and ears went flat. Lazarus snickered. Grace grinned. Aileen blushed and turned herself into a Security goon.

She'd probably end up telling her sister that she had played piano in a whore house when all this was done, rather than admit her parts in the revolution.

She paused and took everyone in.

"Briston, hands together in front of you like you are cuffed," she ordered the guy.

At least he complied without complaint. Points for being willing to take orders from a woman. Most Yithadreph had a different opinion on that sort of things, which was why she was still single while her sister continued making her an auntie.

"Grace and Lazarus after that. Lucas at the rear. Everyone else in the middle somewhere, marching like troops, okay?" Aileen called to the group.

Nobody would fall for it for long, but someone walking up to them might just stand there, jaws agape, long enough for someone to shoot the fool.

She had survived dumber things. Aileen figured this might make the top ten, but maybe not even the top five right now.

However, the day was still young.

Everyone was in place, ready to exit this dock and

penetrate the station itself. Addison had taken command of the security console. Cormac was on the bridge.

Aileen took a deep breath.

"Addison, sound a general alarm," Aileen called to him. "Cormac, open fire."

TWENTY-SIX

LAZARUS

LAZARUS WAS MARCHING at the head of a double column of Human troops like they belonged here. Aileen and her prisoner led and it even looked normal, at least until you realized that the people coming at you were Humans.

Aileen and Briston moved at a rapid pace for Yithadreph, but not even a jog for his long legs. Around them, various alarms hooted and screamed. People were moving every which way, but hardly any paused in what they were doing to question the column of killers moving around.

If you looked like you know what you are doing in an emergency, people tend to assume you did and left you alone.

At least until you got someplace interesting and ran into someone intending to keep you out.

Four times, the hull had rung like a bell. Most of these sailors would not recognize the sound or the vibrations in their feet, but Lazarus had been in enough battles to know the feel of beams slamming into hull and liberating all that energy explosively. The whole vessel would bong.

Hopefully, Cormac had managed to kill the peak of the Pyramid, where all the important people worked and lived.

And then used a Star Spear at boar-fighting range to pick off any turret capable of depressing far enough to hit *Kilri*.

Nobody could use shields with the ship physically docked so beams would be on raw steel, and Innruld metallurgy wasn't up to Rio weapons standards.

A few vac alarms would be useful now, but only to distract. The last thing they needed was for bulkhead locks to start slamming shut and isolating portions of the ship against breach.

Lazarus wasn't even sure that an Innruld vessel would do that, come to think of it. That was a warship design, and this was an office building that flew in space. Maybe fire alarms would close some doors?

They turned a corner and Lazarus nearly ran over Aileen and Briston where they had stopped in the middle of the hallway.

"What is this?" an Innruld woman demanded, pointing at Lazarus with one impossibly long finger.

Lazarus shot her. Grace and Aileen shot the two Kdari troopers with the woman.

Looking around, the hallway was empty. He stepped to a hatch and opened it. A Necherle looked up from a console but he was the only person in the room so Lazarus shot him as well.

"Stuff them in here," he ordered.

Hands grabbed limbs and moved them.

Lazarus stepped over the Innruld woman and dialed the beam on his Ares down tight to shoot the console. It exploded in a shower of sparks. He moved to the hallway and smiled.

"Close it up," he said and Lucas did. "Step back."

And he shattered the door controls with a single shot before dialing his pistol back down to angry medicine ball levels of damage.

Briston was still standing there, mouth open, but Aileen shoved his shoulder.

"This is a war, sailor," she growled at him. "Worse is likely to happen. Fall in."

Lazarus took his spot behind her and they kept moving inward.

TWENTY-SEVEN

AILEEN

AILEEN HAD STUDIED THE MAP, counting corridors and corners, so she knew that her destination was right around this next turn. She considered stopping to ask Lazarus, but she had practically demanded the right to lead, so she needed to pretend like she was management now and decide herself.

She grabbed Briston's arm to stop him in place and turned to the angry storks behind her.

"Next right is our goal," she said quietly, even with the alarms screaming everywhere. "You wait here and watch to see if I can bluff my way close."

"You sure?" Lazarus asked.

"No, but doing it anyway," she replied. "Cover my tail."

He nodded and she lightly shoved Briston into motion. Around the corner, the control center they wanted was on the left hand side. A Zentra and another Yithadreph guarded it, standing passively immobile, flanking a hatch, but with rifles grounded like this was a parade formation.

Aileen walked right close, reaching into a pocket of her

stolen uniform and pulling out the woman's identity papers like they meant something.

"Stop here," she ordered Briston, turning him to face the guards.

"What's this?" the Zentra asked a little sideways.

He had two stripes on his arm instead of the one the Yithadreph had, so apparently he was in charge.

"Prisoner transfer," Aileen announced, like it was the most natural thing in the galaxy in the middle of a firefight and revolution. She held up the papers but didn't hold them out.

The Zentra reached a hand for them, like he was going to read things, so Aileen shoved Briston into the man and pivoted to her right to shoot the Yithadreph.

Briston had apparently been expecting something, because he tackled the Zentra around the legs. It was probably accidental that Briston had hold of the rifle as the man tried to lift it, or keep standing.

Something.

Anything.

Stunner would catch Briston at this point, so she fell back on Xiuying's lessons and punched the man, falling out of the sky like a comet to deliver the blow and ending on her knees with a sickening crack as the guy's eyes rolled back.

Briston's eyes were HUGE as he rolled over and looked at her. Aileen grimaced.

"Humans are dangerous creatures," she said as she stood. "But they are on our side. Keep that in mind."

He nodded and she gave him a hand up. Briston grabbed a rifle as Aileen looked over and saw the rest of her team flooding around the corner. Lucas grinned as he approached.

"Gonna tell Xiuying you did that," he said with a chuckle.

Aileen growled a little under her breath but didn't reply. She turned to Lazarus instead.

"Now what?" she asked the lead stork.

"Now, we need to flood the room beyond this," he said simply. "You two guard our tails, because we're going in and shooting everything that moves and isn't Human. Vectors have already been assigned."

She nodded and grabbed the spare rifle.

"Briston, strip this guy and put his uniform on," she said. "You and I can keep watch out here for now."

Lazarus did something and ALL THE HUMANS came to perfect stillness. Scary. Silent.

One of the engineers stepped to the hatch controls and looked at everyone with a sharp nod.

"Go," Lazarus said, and the man opened the hatch to the primary auxiliary control center for the Pyramid.

Aileen had an impression of a stampede of giant herbivores racing past, except that they weren't any of them really tame or friendly. Maybe a pack of sturee hunting?

Beamfire. Cries of surprise. Screams. Shouts. More beams.

She turned to keep watch on the hallway as a Human apocalypse named Lazarus of Bethany descended on the Innruld.

TWENTY-EIGHT

RODRIGO

HE MIGHT BE AN ADMIRAL, but Rodrigo occasionally missed sitting in the big chair and giving orders. Having Akeley and Capantzina in front of him was a little weird, but both had proven themselves starkly professional during his time around them, and he would happily take them on any future command where he raised his flag.

"Pilot, what is your status?" Rod asked, mostly as a placeholder.

Nothing had changed in the last ten minutes, but the mark of a sharp crew like this one was the ability to tune themselves just a little out of focus while waiting, ready to snap to rather than drifting off somewhere and getting lost when the hat dropped.

"All systems nominal, Admiral," Akeley replied immediately, her ears twitching upright for just a moment before flopping back over. "Jump drives charged and standing by."

"Fusilier, what is your status?" Rod continued, marveling at the weird way those feet drummed the deck around his nest. Right rear forward up the right side, then left front and all the way back down that side. It was almost a counter-clockwise current swirling around the creature. Man. Warrior.

Sailor. Rod didn't have a higher recommendation than *sailor*. And Wybert of Capantzina was a sailor.

"All beams charged and locked, Admiral," he replied by the book. "Shields forward for combat engagement. Forward crew withdrawn to safe quarters for the duration."

Rod nodded. Exactly by the book.

He opened a comm aft.

"Engineering," H'Brige Slani answered instantly.

"We are two minutes to jump," Rod announced, just in case it was possible someone back there didn't have the countdown clock echoed on their screens right now. "Standby to fast charge Kirov's Lance for a second shot."

"Standing by, bridge," she replied. "We'll bring all non-essential systems down when we jump and lock them out for four minutes, or until the battle is over."

"Very well," Rod said and cut the line.

His original orders called for Rodrigo da Silva to make contact with the Innruld and open diplomatic relations, but Councilor Teixeira had amended those to jump straight to revolution. However, Pedro Santos would probably still court martial his sorry ass if he didn't at least pay lip service to those original orders.

So *Ajax* was about to land right on top of an Innruld Security Pyramid and let them have the first volley. Even Slani had been confident that Innruld Powerbolt weapons, the most common thing they had, were nothing but a nuisance.

Rod watched the clock.

"Pilot, you have the helm," he said. "Jump us on the mark. Fusilier, remember that they are allowed the first shot before you return fire."

Both acknowledged with wry grins over their shoulders, just like Human crew who might be telling him—only in their minds, you understand—to teach his grandmother to suck eggs.

Rod grinned back. *Pancho* absolutely had been watched over by God Himself to have met Addison's crew when he discovered Innruld Space. They were good people.

"All hands, transition imminent." Akeley announced over the public address system.

The universe twitched and *Ajax* stepped onto the field of battle.

Capantzina did something loudly on his console, slamming a hand down when he should normally be quietly pressing buttons.

"Alert Override!" he called, that high-pitched voice coming out of every speaker. "All guns crews stand down but remain ready to engage. I have locked you out from the bridge until further notice."

"What's going on?" Rod roared at the man who should be getting ready to commit a mass casualty incident.

Capantzina turn his head to look, and brought something up on the main screen at the same time.

Rod noted a red dot highlighted on one corner of the Pyramid, with an identification transponder marking it as *Star of Kilri*. The top of the Pyramid was a smoking mess, as were several other spots on the hull.

"What the hell?" Rod asked.

"That is why I cannot engage immediately, sir," Capantzina replied with a nod. "I don't know where my friends are, but I suggest we open a hail and find out. Perhaps the Innruld are already prepared to surrender."

TWENTY-NINE

LAZARUS

LAZARUS LOOKED AROUND THE CHAOS. At least he had been right about one wild-ass guess going in. Rio Alliance beam weapons tuned down from a tight, killing beam to something with physical impact were generally safe to just knock most Species on their asses and maybe out cold, without potentially-lethal injuries.

They had brought nearly a thousand plastic restraints, having used up a significant amount of Aileen's sheet stock once they identified their goal, so all the folks in here were bound. Most of them were just knocked goofy, with a few broken limbs but no broken heads.

He'd killed enough people over a lifetime to take some level of comfort in the fact that most of these people would probably be able to return home when he was done.

"Aileen, what do we know?" he called to her.

The outer hatch was closed and she and Briston had pulled those two guards in and added them to the heap tied up in the corner under watch. His Quartermaster was putting her brains to use on a computer system that had been left unlocked when Lazarus had shot the Innruld male seated at it.

Whoops.

She looked up at him now with shock etched on her face. Ears completely flat. Whiskers so far back that it looked painful. Eyes huge.

"What?" Lazarus asked, immediately moving towards her. The others could cover things.

She pointed mutely at the screen, mouth opening and closing without sound, so Lazarus moved around her to see what she was looking at.

Wow.

It was a damage control readout. Of the Pyramid.

The top was missing. Just *gone.*

When they'd shot the ziggurat on Gowook, it had been a concrete building built to look the same externally, but had been concrete with stone facings. Heavy pillars designed to uphold all that weight safely.

He'd forgotten that the Innruld didn't build things so durable in space. Didn't need to, since a ship like this could never land on the surface of a planet.

"Who's in charge of the Pyramid now?" Lazarus asked.

It sure as hell wasn't the original bridge. That was just a red spot on her damage control map, possibly vented to deep space.

"I think we are," she said.

Her voice was tiny, but he still heard it over the alarms.

Lazarus took a deep breath and studied the console. He killed the alarms in here so he could think better and looked closer.

Yes, this space had taken over at the moment when all signals from the top of the Pyramid had ceased. Right now, until someone else figured out what was going on, he was in command of the vessel.

"What happens if you give the command to abandon ship?" he asked her as silence suddenly descended on them.

Aileen looked up in confusion for a moment, and then nodded.

"Every ship at Oton Mari Station is supposed to immediately launch in a search and rescue mission to find all the pods," she said. "This close to Oton Mari, the pods themselves will either home in on the station or start to go for planetary descent, depending on where they are."

"But everyone would be gone?" he pressed.

"Yeah, I think." Finally, her face got sly and the smile came back. "Yes, they would be gone."

"Do it," he told her.

Lazarus watched the woman take a deep breath and turn back to her new console, pressing various buttons.

"All hands abandon ship," she said in a calm, authoritative voice. "Repeat, all hands. This vessel is unstable and will explode imminently. Abandon ship."

She did something else and that started to loop out of the speakers, but she had turned them down in here so it was more like listening to the radio than the apocalypse. A moment later, she must have opened a comm line. Lazarus smiled as he watched her work.

"Oton Mari Station, we are declaring an emergency," Aileen said. "Launch all vessels to recover escape pods. I repeat, launch all of your vessels to recover our escape pods."

She looked up at him. Smiled.

"That is now officially the biggest, meanest practical joke I have ever played on anybody," she said. "Hopefully, we don't kill too many people with this stunt."

"The alternative was that we had to kill this entire ship when *Ajax* arrived," Lazarus reminded her. "Here, most of them will get away. And they can carry that message of fear and surprise home with them to infect other places. That goes a long ways towards eroding the sense of Innruld invincibility before the first shot is ever fired in some places."

Lazarus fell to silence as he listened to the hull start ringing to an entirely different note. Escape pods, blasting clear once everyone was aboard. He looked at a screen and watched a cloud of gnats suddenly engulf this Pyramid.

"Hey, there's *Ajax*," Aileen said. "Right on time. Wow, we were early on everything, weren't we?"

Lazarus looked at the local time and felt his mouth fall open a little.

"Yeah," he agreed. "But they never knew what hit them, so we were able to strike right to their heart."

"Now what do we do?" she asked.

"Open a line to Rod, first and foremost," Lazarus said. "Then we'll have Briston talk to his people once all the craziness winds down."

"So we can start it all right back up?" Aileen asked, her smile pulled a little sideways.

"You wanted a revolution, kid," Lazarus growled at her. "This is it."

THIRTY

RODRIGO

RODRIGO STUDIED the mess and shook his head. Ticks running like hell as the dog was about to get a chemical bath time.

"Sir, we're being hailed by the Pyramid," Akeley called out. "I have Aileen on line. Visual as well as audio."

"Put her on the main screen, Lt. Commander," Rod replied.

Aileen and Lazarus both, crowded in a little to be in the shot. Smiling.

"By now, you've scanned the escape pods, Admiral," Lazarus said. "We sounded the alert to abandon ship here once we took over the secondary bridge. My recommendation to you would be to withdraw some, as everyone on the main station is legally required to come rescue, and a few might get too close to you for comfort."

"Pilot, back us out and bring us around to where we have both the Pyramid and the Station in front of us, but well off to one side," Rod said, trusting Akeley to figure out what he needed. She was good at that. "Lazarus, now what?"

"We own the Pyramid, sir," *Pancho* replied. "From here

we threaten the station to surrender and we've just doubled our firepower, instead of having to destroy the Pyramid to make our point."

"How did you manage to damage that thing so badly, *Pancho?*"

"That was a Star Spear, Admiral da Silva," the man turned serious. "Fired point blank from a stable platform, without shields. I believe I mentioned that Innruld vessels are not up to Rio Alliance standards as warships?"

"You did, Lazarus," Rod joined the man in seriousness. "I do not think I really believed you until this moment."

"The Kirov Lance, aimed just right, could quite possibly blow Oton Mari Station into about five major components, Admiral," Lazarus continued, eyes and voice deadly. "With sufficient kinetic force imparted from the explosion that most of them would probably deorbit fairly quickly. Hopefully, it will not be necessary."

"Hopefully, you are correct, Captain," Rod agreed. "What are your orders?"

He liked the way Lazarus blinked and maybe flinched a little, but he was the man in charge over there. *Ajax* was just the galaxy's biggest freaking hammer, but there were no nails that needed driving at the moment.

At the moment.

On one of his smaller screens, Rod watched ships start to depart from Oton Mari Station. A few freighters but mostly small mining craft. On the one hand, no small miner could rescue more than a single pod, but they also had waldo arms designed for holding and manipulating asteroids and rocks, so there might not be a better design to capture an escape pod and get it to safety.

Whatever safety there might be, with the Sword of Damocles hanging off on a flank, ready to annihilate the station should they give him a good enough reason.

"Fusilier, stand down," Rod ordered. "Do a hard scan of all escape pods and keep a running tally of any that do not appear to be in the process of being rescued. Broadcast your list on a clear channel regularly. Take charge of vectoring in any vessels that ask, but we will not allow any vessels to approach *Ajax*. Warn them off if they try."

"And if they refuse to withdraw?" Capantzina asked.

"We'll burn that bridge when we get there, Fusilier."

THIRTY-ONE

OLUCHI

OLUCHI HAD SOMEHOW BEEN APPOINTED *in loco parentis* as a stand-in for Addison today, much to his surprise. But he supposed that it made sense. Not counting Lazarus, who was also forced to be absent, he had known Eha the longest among all the Humans in the galaxy.

It had been Oluchi's legs that a panicked Eha had wrapped herself around when they were escaping Strav Ardna's yacht, just before Lazarus and friends blew it to hell. Still, he had absolutely no idea what he was supposed to be doing here, other than standing firm as a male presence which was apparently a cultural thing.

Eha was in a nest at the center of the room, a Churquen thing that served the same purpose as a hospital bed, for a species without legs. Alla was on one side, and a female doctor whose name Oluchi had managed to forget in the heat of the moment was on the other. Two nurses—female and male—came and went, doing medical things that eluded him completely.

Oluchi patiently stood a long stride back from the nest as he watched, careful not to move as there were two and sometimes five tails on the floor that he might accidentally step on. Or trip over.

"Shortly," the doctor announced in a calmer voice than anyone else in the room.

But she was a professional. Eha was in a mild amount of pain, but nothing like a Human mother. Alla was a little frazzled, but holding it all inside, except when her tail kinked ninety degrees every few minutes.

The nurses slithered close and Oluchi had a hard time seeing anything through the thing he could only compare to a true snake ball.

At least Churquen gave birth to live young. He'd been originally worried that Eha would be laying an egg and watching over it, but apparently the species had moved past that in the evolutionary past.

One child, according to the woman in charge as doctor. Healthy and a little feisty, according to Eha's commentary this last week as the little one wriggled inside her, getting ready to be born.

Eha was coiled with her lower body on its side and her torso more or less upright. There was some pain on her face.

The doctor suddenly grabbed Oluchi by a hand and pulled him closer.

"Here," the woman said. "Make yourself useful and hold her hand."

Somehow, Oluchi managed to not step on anyone as he got to the edge of the nest.

Eha held out a hand and he could see how all her scales were flared out now around her face and even her neck. Pain or anticipation was hard to tell, because he'd never seen this particular pattern to those scales.

Her head came around as she squeezed his hands, not that she had the strength to hurt him. But he was there to give her someone to concentrate on, so he smiled.

Eha rippled. Oluchi couldn't find a better term to describe it. It seemed to start at her shoulders and went right down her body to the spot just below where her slithering half normally touched keelscales with the ground when she moved.

He could see an opening there now, and supposed that it was the Churquen equivalent of a Human's vagina.

How the hell had an ex-gigolo like him ended up watching a Churquen Ambassador give birth? Did the universe get much weirder?

No, don't ask that too loudly. Someone might take it as a challenge.

She spasmed again, maybe with a little more pain this time because her other hand came up and caught his. Oluchi held both of hers in his.

They were back in the water off the stern of Cardinal, with him providing her a rock around which to coil as she fought off panic. Oluchi didn't think Eha was panicking right now, but she was also a first-time mother, so all of this would be almost as new to her as it was to him.

He concentrated on her eyes, trying to mesmerize her into focusing on him. It seemed to work.

"You're doing fine," he said, even as the four Churquen around him were all chattering quietly at each other, most of it medical talk that went right over his head.

Another convulsion wracked her body and Oluchi heard the doctor speak clearly.

"It has begun," she said. "One or two more and you'll be done."

A fourth spasm and Eha found the strength to squeeze his hands like her body had bruised his legs on Yisan's sea.

More encouragement from the other end of the nest, but Oluchi ignored it. There were some things that he really didn't need to see, and he was pretty sure watching a Churquen give birth was one of them.

Even if she was one of his closest friends in the universe.

He let her hold on and one final push seemed to exhaust her. Alla and the others cheered. Oluchi found himself more or less holding Eha upright, but Alla popped up and leaned against his shoulder like a constrictor about to have lunch.

"She needs to lay down now," Alla said quietly. "Carefully."

So Oluchi let her down. Eha ended up more or less flat on her back, so he moved to his left to keep himself near her head. Her eyes were closed, but all she had to do was open them and look a little to her right and he'd be there for her. That was about as good a promise as he could make.

The doctor had a bundle in her hands, wrapped up in a towel. No, a blanket. She moved next to Oluchi and stretched a newborn Churquen, about eighteen inches long, out on Eha's chest to bond.

The species weren't mammals, so Eha had no breasts to feed the youngster. Instead, they had once regurgitated food like birds, but now just had a dry, lumpy gruel that they could feed the baby by hand.

"Boy or girl?" Oluchi asked.

Apparently, even modern Innruld science wasn't able to gender a Churquen child *in utero*, so they had to do that when the kit was born. Eha opened her eyes and wrapped her hands protectively around the little body wriggling on her stomach for a comfortable spot.

The doctor laid the blanket across both of them and smiled at him.

"Girl," she announced. "Just as feisty as her mother and grandmother."

"Good," Oluchi replied.

He turned to take in the historic image of the first

Churquen birth on a Rio Alliance world, and what it would mean for the future.

"Which name did you finally settle on?" he asked Eha when she smiled up at him, exhausted but exhilarated from the way her eyeslits were resting.

"Adriana," she said.

"Is that a Churquen name?" Oluchi asked, surprised.

"No," Eha replied with a cryptic smile. "It is a Rio name, for my daughter born in the Rio Alliance."

THIRTY-TWO

CARLOS

CARLOS KNEW that big things were happening on the ground, but he needed to be up on the station, meeting with Lazarus's two allies that he had left in charge, Governor Garcia and Security Chief Bălan. Commander Rodriguez was also present, representing the original escort force for *Ajax* that had been deployed here to protect the station.

There were others he could have insisted on coming, but Carlos wanted this small and intimate, at least for now as he looked at the others.

Garcia was a lower decks engineer. A career chief who had never even been to officer candidate school, but she was holding a position that a Commander would have been slotted into. Lazarus had been desperate and in a hurry, but he'd picked well.

Still, that meant that Carlos was the senior officer in the system right now, at least as those things were measured. Garcia was Governor and had a battle station under her command, so perhaps that made her his peer.

Too much unknown.

"*Dutra* is a Patrol Cruiser," he began, reminding them

that Admiral da Silva had originally ordered him to stay put only as long as was necessary before heading back into Innruld Space. "We are barely more heavily armed than a destroyer, so not of much use in a battle if Westphalia decides to return. But I get the feeling that things have changed since I was originally ordered here."

"We originally expected the station would provide an extra anchor point in the defensive line," Bălan spoke up now. "But that was before you arrived, Captain. Now we have probably been upgraded to a major target that Westphalia needs to attack before everything gets so settled and reinforced that they can't hope to win."

"You have a station," Carlos pointed out.

"In geo-synched orbit of Four," Garcia reminded him, in case he had forgotten. "They can still do whatever they wanted at Five, or even Seven where the original battle was fought. Without the Kirov Lance and that deadly Ilount wielding it, we would need a fleet to stop them from bringing their own fleet in. A station can be defeated, given time and patience, and the random squadron around here is just that, random."

"And you've sent requests for more help?" Carlos asked, again, like he had forgotten, hoping that maybe some new detail might come up.

Garcia just nodded.

"The most recent one notified Fleet and presumably the High Council that we had refugees, with dates and details," she said. "But I don't know how quickly they will react. You know how politicians are."

Carlos grimaced. Fleet Admirals were almost as bad as senior politicians that way, but getting to flag rank was a political thing. One he was unlikely to ever achieve, but Carlos was happier flying *Dutra* than anything.

"What does the arrival of Adriana Dunham do to the

equation?" Bălan asked now. "That's a highly symbolic thing, far in excess of just the colony. Now it is growing, and the first birth would always be important, but it was the Ambassador herself."

They all nodded. Lazarus was willing to ignore orders and do things because he thought they were right, but he also had long since stopped caring if and when they hauled his ass up in front of a Court Martial. *Pancho* Oliveira had died and been reborn as *Lazarus of Bethany*.

Carlos Nguema didn't have anything similar going, except conviction based on thirty years in uniform.

"Cavalry time," he said simply.

"*Dutra?*" Bălan asked, brightening.

Carlos nodded.

"What am I missing?" Garcia asked.

"We have both Ambassadors present, plus a High Councilor, several Yisan oligarchs, and a newborn Churquen daughter," Carlos said. "I've got Marie Oslor and her team back, which brings me back up to full strength, since I left so many engineers with *Ajax* when we left. Near as I can tell, we need to get Teixeira back to Brasilia so she can light a fire under some asses, and we need Admiral Santos to decide that the time has come to mount a rescue. They've politely ignored junior officers arriving in pinckes, except to file the message and pat them on the head. They can't ignore *Dutra* as well."

"Weren't your orders to return to da Silva?" Bălan asked.

"Technically, but only in the context of assisting him in his patrol and exploration mission," Carlos nodded. "His mission will work far better if I can get you help here. Now, while it is still good and not after Westphalia drops a significant force in here and takes everyone prisoner, maybe killing them or just hauling them off to a prison world behind Westphalia lines. I can always run like hell for

Akeley's Passage later, since nobody but me has ever sailed it properly."

"Gonna go rogue if Santos says no?" Bălan smiled. Garcia joined him a moment later.

"Already rogue, Commanders," Carlos grinned. "Might have to get serious about it."

"What do you need from me?" **Governor** Garcia asked.

"Most recent sitrep, including the birth announcement," Carlos said. "Plus we need to convince the key players to depart with us, and I'm not sure they will."

"Eha will," Bălan said. "The others probably. What do you do about the oligarchs?"

"Invite them to bring a chef along and pack my stores with better food than the fleet provides," Carlos laughed. "While providing them transport to Brasilia for political discussions."

"Is that yacht armed?" Garcia asked.

"Not legally," Carlos replied. "But I also haven't scanned it from close range to tell. If a battle breaks out while I'm gone, they might be able to contribute, but I'd be surprised if they did. More likely just withdraw and maybe return to Yisan to await orders."

She grimaced and Carlos felt sympathy. Any gun would probably be useful if Westphalia returned.

"Anything else?" he asked, but they didn't have any more good ideas.

Carlos nodded as they broke up the meeting to start preparation.

Cavalry time. Hopefully, he could convince the major players to move.

THIRTY-THREE

EDUARDO

EDUARDO CONSIDERED TELLING the Gnashiiley captain the truth about *Celestial Sovereign*, his yacht, but decided to let it slide. Out beyond the borders of Westphalia or the Rio Alliance, things could be less... civilized, so his little yacht was a pocket escort possibly comparable to the two Protector warships already in orbit.

He watched out of *Dutra*'s porthole as the ship went through a jump, all the stars suddenly redshifting around him. Turning back to the cabin he was in, Eduardo smiled. Had they taken *Celestial Sovereign* everything would have been more comfortable, but he did agree that the locals at Brasilia would have been less inclined to listen.

So he was in an officer's cabin on a Rio Patrol Cruiser. His closet, back on Yisan, was larger, to say nothing of his bathroom. But this was a warship, and you needed to build them as compact as possible, offsetting weight and durability against comfort.

A knock at the hatch. Eduardo took all of four steps to open it, marveling that he had allowed himself to be talked into this, but the future of the galaxy itself would be shaped by this vessel. At least the Gnashiiley captain had been wise enough to bring all the key players, even if Eduardo was almost certain he could hear Leena ranting about the accommodations, even from three rooms away.

He smiled and opened the hatch to find Marie standing there. Dressed in uniform again, but looking more relaxed than he remembered from her time on Yisan or Vilga.

"Captain Nguema is having a planning meeting and hopes you will be able to join him," she said obliquely.

As in, now. As in, jump, but phrased politely.

Eduardo glanced around and nodded.

"After you, Lieutenant Oslor," he smiled at the woman.

She returned it and led him through a variety of corridors and down a level to a larger meeting room, arriving just as Captain Nguema did.

Inside, Eduardo noted that the group was rather pared down from what he might have expected. Councilor Teixeira. Oluchi and Anya. Fernanda Flores. Ambassador Dunham with daughter Adriana in a small bassinet, presumably asleep for now. Marie Oslor took a chair along a wall, but Captain Nguema brought her up to the table.

Eduardo noted that Collin and Leena had not been invited, nor were there other aides besides Marie present. Interesting. Just the key players, then?

The Gnashiiley Captain studied everyone quickly before he spoke. The room was large enough to have held three times the number, with a rectangular conference table and magnetic chairs, plus more chairs around the outside of the room. Eduardo noted a refrigerator in one corner, along with a coffee stand. A door to a bathroom was next to it, so presumably one could hold a major, long-term planning meeting here.

Eduardo disliked chairs in meeting rooms. On Yisan, all

the tables were tall enough for someone to stand at, with step-shelves if an attendee was exceptionally short.

If you had to stand, the meetings did not drag. People did not lean back and let their minds wander. Business was conducted fast and then everyone went about their ways.

The Rio Alliance Navy apparently had yet to learn that lesson from the civilian world.

"Our goal, my hope that is, is to get to Brasilia fast and convince them to upgrade Vilga from a backwater to a major base and port," Captain Nguema began. "All of you are here because you have some facet of the overall picture that you can contribute. High Councilor Teixeira, am I chasing a pipe dream?"

Eduardo noted the woman, and how much physical resemblance there was to Fernanda. Both had obviously been amazing women in athletic shape well past their fifties, and still looked good. Vibrant. Intellectual. Especially compared to an old harridan like Leena.

Skin tone and hair color was really all that separated these two women.

Erlyn Teixeira studied him in return as she ordered her thoughts. Eduardo wondered what she saw. He had twenty-five years on her, and was tall and portly, but he had done all his crazy, stupid things before he was forty, and then settled in for corporate warfare fought from behind a desk.

"I believe the arrival of the embassy from Yisan indicates just how seriously some players take the situation," Teixeira began, still watching him. "Three major oligarchs, plus their Ambassador to Brasilia. The offer of tighter social, economic, and political ties will certainly get attention."

She turned to Eha while Eduardo watched Teixeira's face for clues.

"Further, I believe that we can, at least for now and in this room, dispense with the suggestion that we do not know how to reach Innruld Space," Teixeira continued. "I am confident enough to say that as seen from Brasilia, the trade route will pass close to Yisan itself, and probably pass right though the center of any polity based on Yisan. Actual coordinates are less important as we talk, but Yisan is the doorway to Innruld Space, and Planetary Governor Alla Dunham, Adriana's grandmother, is likely to be the key."

"Do we believe that Westphalia knows the way?" Oluchi spoke up. "After all, they sent a ScoutWall into the Nebula and encountered *Dutra* there. How soon will they discover Akeley's Passage?"

Eduardo noted the stirring around the room. But then, Oluchi was always far, far smarter than he let on, possibly even to himself. Eduardo had never been fooled.

"I instructed the captains of the two vessels I chartered to take the safest route possible home." Eduardo leaned forward now, resting his elbows on the tabletop and glancing right to left to catch all eyes. "To take their time and calculate every jump three times, just so there were no accidents. As they were being paid charter rates on a daily contingency, I am confident that they did not immediately race to Westphalian space. If anything, they might take their time sailing directly to Earth itself."

"How long does that buy us?" Captain Nguema asked.

"From point of departure, I'm guessing roughly ninety days," Eduardo nodded to the man. "Any longer and it would have become obvious that I had ordered the delay."

"And from there, they will have to approach their own fleet command and presumably the Executive," Fernanda spoke up now. "If I have read the reports correctly, they made it only about half-way though the Nebula when you had encountered them, Captain?"

All eyes turned to the Gnashiiley.

"That's right," he said, nodding. "I got the impression

from Lazarus that we were past mid-point, and actually pretty close to emerging from the far side, but that would have required another passage and the ScoutWall didn't have a chance to start exploring for it. But they can get that far with a fleet."

"Won't do them any good," Eha said now. "That system has long been a place for smugglers to meet because it is so difficult to access from the Innruld side. Lazarus should have hit a gravity well in his jump and died. How difficult was it for you, Captain, to make it there?"

"Extremely," Nguema agreed. "Which brings me to the key point that I don't think people have really grasped so far, but I had a lot of time to explore those possibilities on the flight to Vilga."

He paused, and Eduardo had to appreciate that hesitation. It was like sitting at the poker table with the man, just waiting for him to call on the last raise. Eduardo considered starting a very low-stakes poker game with some of these people. Oluchi was here and expert. Fernanda could generally hold her own. There must be a game down in the crew section that would offer some challenge, if not much in the way of real stakes.

"Westphalia will decide that they have a problem, when the crews of that ScoutWall get home," Nguema continued. "They didn't find the way, and still have to conclude that Rio or someone will probably do what they can to secure it, possibly by building a forward base or a series of them, from whence they can pounce on Westphalia support ships sailing back and forth."

"That is a reasonable assumption, Captain," Eduardo said when the man turned to look at him. "We have considered how it might be done, and when, but felt that we needed a formal treaty with both the Species Underground as well as the Rio Alliance before we took such a step. Too easy for things to be misconstrued."

"Yes, but they don't have to guess now, do they?" Nguema smiled.

"What do you mean?" Teixeira asked.

"If they capture Vilga, there are nine ships and several dozen people there who know the way through to Innruld Space," Nguema said. "All they have to do is invade and capture them. After that, they might even find a faster way around the nebula."

"Around?" Eduardo asked, appalled at the waste of time that might entail.

But Nguema smiled.

"The galactic disk is only about one thousand light-years thick," he said. "And most of that is within about one hundred and fifty light-years of the exact plane. The farther out you go, the less chance of hitting things, so you might be able to take a tremendous leap straight up or down, then hop sideways, then inward again, and do it faster than going across."

Eduardo felt a shock ripple through his whole body as he leaned back. Fernanda felt it. Oluchi, too. Anya Persaud gave nothing away.

Nguema nodded.

"Patrol Cruisers work in three dimensions," he continued. "Most people think in two, maybe with levels. If Westphalia knows where they are going, there's really nothing to stop them from getting there."

"There is one, thing, Captain," Eduardo felt it necessary to point out right now.

"What's that?" the Gnashiiley asked brightly, inquisitive rather than combative.

"We could simply overthrow Westphalia, Captain

Nguema," Eduardo stated boldly. Baldly. "Then they are not a threat to peace, trade, or development."

"The Rio Alliance is barely holding their own, Martìnez," Nguema replied. "*Ajax* was an attempt to break the stalemate."

"Indeed," Eduardo agreed. "What happens if Yisan and all our allies come in on your side?"

Bedlam, but he had been expecting that. It still took several minutes for people to settle.

"Why would you do that?" Nguema finally asked the billion credit question. "Why would Yisan suddenly take sides, when all you have to do is sit back and trade?"

"Westphalia wouldn't allow it," Eduardo said. "So I need to make sure that I am on the winning side, and then ram that point home as painfully as necessary."

He took a deep breath as the bedlam erupted again, but it felt right.

Eduardo Martìnez probably wouldn't live to see it succeed, but he could already identify how quickly it would fail if nothing was done.

So he was going to do something about it.

THIRTY-FOUR

ANYA

ANYA HAD BEEN a spy for nearly fifteen years. Little stuff, going undercover as part of her job working for various Ministries and Planning Departments, where she could serve as a fresh pair of eyes that weren't beholden to the official channels that *managed* information flowing up the food chain.

Unedited data, which was occasionally deeply at odds with official statements.

But that was the past. She stood outside this hatch and contemplated the future. Her future.

Ex-spy, identity irrevocably blown now and more or less put out to pasture, as she had once told Oluchi was to be her expected fate. She just hadn't expected it to occur at thirty-six.

Anya knocked.

The hatch opened and Erlyn smiled at her, gesturing her into the tiny cabin the woman had. Anya was getting used to sleeping in extremely trying circumstances. At least she had her own cabin, so she didn't have to try actually *sleeping* with Oluchi on a bunk meant for one person.

But neither Erlyn nor Eduardo had any better, at least until *Dutra* arrived at Brasilia.

Erlyn silently gestured her to the chair and closed the hatch, before moving to sit on the bottom end of the bunk.

"So what brings you, Anya?" she asked. "I was a bit surprised by the request for a private meeting."

"I've been thinking," Anya replied. "Scheming, planning, evaluating, whatever you want to call it. I can't go home."

"There are no warrants out for your arrest that I'm aware of," Erlyn grinned. "What have you and your sidekick been doing that I am not aware of?"

Anya couldn't help but grin. She respected Erlyn. Liked her. Occasionally filtered things she wanted to do through the image of Teixeira as a role model.

"I can't be a happy little cog in the depths of the bureaucracy," Anya replied. "It was always a given that eventually I was likely to be discovered."

"And you have a full pension," Erlyn reminded her. "You will not be wanting for money, so I presume that you have other qualms?"

"Eduardo has asked if I would be interested in a position somewhere in his organization," Anya said. "Oluchi kind of invited himself in, and that's all still rather nebulous, but I need to be more than just Pryce's girlfriend."

"Are there personal issues I need to be aware of?" Erlyn asked, suddenly far more serious.

"No," Anya said flatly. "That part of my life is actually doing well. Oluchi has danced around the topic, and so have I, but there is likely to be some sort of long-term partnership in that direction, at least on a personal basis."

"Okay?" Erlyn replied, mostly as a placeholder.

"At one point, I jokingly asked Fernanda for one hundred million credits to start purchasing or building companies involved in upgrading Innruld and the Species to Rio standards," Anya explained. "Except that I'm not sure she was kidding when she said maybe. Nor Eduardo. These people have so much money available that it is more like oxygen, only notable if it were to suddenly vanish."

"I see," Erlyn said. "So what do you want out of life, Anya?"

"I want to be a power player," Anya decided. "Oluchi saw the chance at the brass ring, and grabbed hold. He's told me how scared shitless he's been a few times at his luck and audacity. He keeps expecting to wake up and be back on Yisan, seducing people like Leena."

They both shuddered. The woman was shrill, complaining about nearly everything. Anya had wondered more than once if she was just lonely for a Dom who could really abuse her without leaving visible marks, according to some of the things Oluchi had mentioned in passing.

When Erlyn didn't speak, Anya took a deep breath and plowed on.

"Right now, I feel like I have to make it clear to you and maybe the rest of the Rio government that I won't necessarily be on your side when it starts settling down again." Anya tried to find the right words. "Eduardo wants me as an expert on Rio government, on his side of the table negotiating, like Oluchi is doing. I've told him that there were certain topics I would never discuss, but I still wanted your opinion. Will the High Council treat me as a foreign ambassador, like they do Oluchi, or will they see me as one of their spies who betrayed them? Do I have to worry about folks on Brasilia sending people like Grace Savidge after me one of these days?"

"Not that I am aware of," Erlyn said quickly, before falling back into thought.

Anya held her counsel close and watched the woman.

"I'm sure there will be hurt feelings," Erlyn finally said. "But those people can be made to understand that you have fully retired, as long as they don't suspect you have sold them out."

"I'm not sure how to convey that to them," Anya grimaced now. "I know many things that some powerful players would rather never came out. Personally embarrassing things. That's why I worry, especially if I no longer can count on Rio to protect me."

"It would have to be a hard, clean rupture," Erlyn said. "The standard resignation letter with a date, after which all things change."

"I'm aware of that, Erlyn," Anya said, marveling that she could call the woman by her given name without a quaver to her voice. "When we get to Brasilia, I want everyone to understand that at most I intend to pack a few things up, sell off or give away a lot of it, and leave a forwarding address somewhere. Possibly Vilga, possibly Yisan. But if you are fine with it, I will date my resignation for when we arrive on Brasilia."

"Make it the day after we land," Erlyn stated emphatically. "That way you are on the ground and they can't get pissy about it and leave you on a station or something. Also, make sure Eduardo or Fernanda have you covered with an employment contract that doesn't leave a gap anywhere."

Anya was a little surprised, but Erlyn smiled.

"You're sure?" she asked.

"I am," Erlyn said. "You've done your job and gone so far above and beyond that Cavalcanti and the rest don't have any grounds to complain."

"And if he does, I might mention names," Anya said slyly.

"Oh?"

"The night we helped Eha escape originally," Anya smiled. "I was leading everyone down the back way when I went to check on a noise and accidentally ran into the old horndog Roald coming out of someone's apartment in the middle of the night."

"Oh, did you now?" Erlyn returned the smile.

"A young administrative aide who most certainly wasn't Mrs Cavalcanti by any stretch of the imagination," Anya said. "If he makes a stink, I'll just remind him. As long as there aren't any ninjas coming after me."

"I'll have a chat with the Council Guards and remind them who they work for," Erlyn turned serious. "Activities against a foreign ambassador qualify as acts of war under all legal systems. They don't want that on their conscience."

"Thank you." Anya rose now.

Erlyn stood as well and Anya found herself being hugged.

"Consider it a wedding present, even if you never make it formal with that scamp," Erlyn laughed. "It is absolutely the least we could do for you, and I'll make sure we do more as things settle. You gave us fifteen years of your life at reasonable risk. You should be allowed to enjoy the rest."

It took a few minutes, and a few more hugs, but eventually Anya found herself standing in the hallway again, butt leaned against a wall as she tried to sort it all out.

Oluchi wanted her. Wanted her around. Wanted to explore all the possibilities that lay before them as partners or unindicted co-conspirators.

Eduardo wanted her just for her mind, but that desire was just as strong on his part.

It would mean giving up nearly everything, but she'd been living a lie for so long that nobody knew the real her. Maybe not even herself.

A war was one hell of a time to go on a quest of self-discovery, but as she stood and started walking, Anya decided that she was looking forward to it.

THIRTY-FIVE

CARLOS

CARLOS ENTERED the office and stood at attention, eyes locating some mid-point between here and Earth. Or Zhoonarrim, depending on which way he was facing.

Admiral Santos seemed to have a look of exhaustion mixed possibly with disgust on his face, but remained silent long enough that Carlos almost got nervous. The desk was a mess, with folders piled and various books opened and stacked so as to have some reference point immediately available.

It was completely unlike anything Carlos was prepared for. Most of the time, an Admiral's desk had a nameplate, a pen, and a coffee mug. Nothing else. Admiral Santos's desk looked as exhausted and overworked as the man himself.

"Sit, Captain," the Chief of the Admiralty said in a tired voice.

Carlos found a spot, thinking to himself how strange the chairs around here were. At least they had been designed for three species with some manner of tail. Gnashiiley tails were nowhere near as big and fancy as Atomarsk. Moah were even stubbier.

But soon they would have to begin investing in all manner of new methods.

At least if everything worked out.

"Last time I spoke to you, you were headed into Innruld Space with Rod," Santos began.

Carlos started to speak but a hand came up to stop him before he did more than take a breath.

"I've read all the reports, Carlos," the Admiral said. "And you're in for a couple of different commendations, personally as well as for your crew. Good job. When you see Rod, tell him he owes you a drink and that I said so."

Carlos felt his ears twitch in embarrassment, but remained silent for now.

"The most recent thing to cross my desk is from Councilor Teixeira," Santos pivoted now. "It related to a conversation you and she were part of on the flight here from Vilga."

Carlos nodded. *That* conversation.

"You are of the opinion that Westphalia will make a major play against Vilga," Admiral Santos stated clearly. "Based on the logic that it gives them the ability to capture Churquen or Yithadreph pilots who can plot courses to Innruld worlds."

"That's right, sir," Carlos finally said. "Everyone thinks of the Nebula as a shield, at least from the Human side. But space is three dimensional and you could probably go around one end or over the top faster than cutting through the middle, but only if you knew where you were going on the far side."

"And you think I should move a squadron or even a small fleet to Vilga as a defensive measure," Santos continued.

"I think that the forces currently in place are not sufficient to hold the system against any significant incursion by Westphalian forces, Admiral," Carlos replied carefully, trying to keep his emotions perfectly flat when he'd rather be yelling right now.

One did not address one's ultimate superior officer in a voice better suited for a bar fight.

Usually.

"Even though *Ajax* mashed the shit out of *Gotland* and two GunWalls last time?" Santos asked. "And you were part of a force that functionally annihilated a ScoutWall?"

"Because of, Admiral," Carlos said. "At some point, their spies are going to tell them about a colony of so-called aliens on Vilga. I'm pretty sure that there weren't any leaks while we were there, so I would measure things by yesterday when *Dutra* transmitted the first reports on a secure channel, even before we docked. Time to disseminate information to the various agencies and departments that need to react. Time to collate a report. Flight time to Earth by whatever shortest route someone might take from here to there, presumably three-hopping from here to a Rio world close to the border, then smuggled across, then run like hell to Earth itself. Assemble a fleet or just throw a squadron at the problem. Flight time to Vilga. Battle."

"You've given this a lot of thought," Santos accused him.

"Started thinking about it ten seconds after the ScoutWall asked for terms, Admiral," Carlos admitted. "We were always going to repatriate those men and women, and they would be able to plot half the course, so I was expecting a larger force to cross next time, but they have the same problem. A ScoutWall is at least designed to sail immense distances and stay at sea for a long time. Westphalia would need to build stations and depots forward, especially as the big dogs from Yisan are talking about throwing a backstop across their flight path."

"So to speak," Santos corrected him.

"So to speak, sir," Carlos agreed. "But the ability to step

through a jump and be anywhere still gets limited by time to find things, so you need freighters along with fresh supplies. If they have to go all the way home each time, you move slower than if you can just hop over to Yisan and refill your bays."

"This does not leave this office, Captain," Admiral Santos got so deadly serious that Carlos did a double take. He nodded. "We have provisionally accepted a deal with Martìnez and Flores that will evolve into a semi-formal treaty, aligning the Rio Alliance with the merchants of Yisan, until such time something more formal is done to create a proper political entity."

Carlos fell back against his seat in shock. His mouth opened and closed with no sound emerging.

Finally, he found his voice.

"Do they have the military force to hold Westphalia off, sir?" he asked. "I thought that they were civilians."

"Let us say that they are comparable to Innruld that way, Captain," the Admiral's smile turned positively feral. "More of a police force than a combat navy, but it also means that they have a tremendous number of small patrol ships that are more heavily armed than their tonnage would normally suggest."

"Flying into a nest of hornets?" Carlos asked.

"Something like that," the man agreed.

"So does that stop Westphalia from taking the direct route with any significant force?" Carlos asked, deciding to hazard a guess now.

"That is the Admiralty's consensus, Carlos," Santos replied. "They might try to send something like *Dutra*, a long-range explorer on a solo mission, or another ScoutWall but nothing significant, and I am willing to gamble that anyone emerging on the far side eventually encounters *Ajax* and hopefully all those guns you left behind when you came back here. That will seal that end of the pipe for now."

"But it still leaves Vilga, sir," Carlos pointed out.

"It does, Captain," Santos said.

Carlos watched the man come to some internal decision now, studying him. Finally, he spoke.

"I must apologize, Carlos," Admiral Santos said quietly. "Normally, this would be a major announcement and grounds for a significant party, but time and the need for secrecy are working against us right now, for all the reasons you have just pointed out."

"Sir?"

Carlos watched the man rifle in the stack on his left before he selected a folder and opened it. He pulled out a piece of paper and carefully signed and dated it as Carlos watched.

Admiral Santos looked up and there was finally a smile on his face.

"Given the situation, I need a commander in place at Vilga who understands the situation, the players, and the stakes, Carlos," Santos said.

The man slid the piece of paper across the desk and turned it right side up.

Carlos looked down and felt his jaw drop open again and his ears come all the way forward.

"You're promoting me to Contra-Almirante, sir?" Carlos looked up in shock. "Rear Admiral?"

Santos nodded and smiled.

"You will take command of the Heavy Starcruiser *Recife*, currently in local orbit, Rear Admiral Nguema," the man continued. "Commander Peláez will brevet to command of *Dutra* for now, while the Admiralty decides if we should make it a permanent gig. *Dutra* will attach to *Recife*'s full squadron and you will make best time to Vilga and take command of all naval forces there, working in concert with Governor Garcia. Formal orders will be cut shortly, routing everyone, but it will be done as quickly and quietly as we can, and you will not tell Captain Quispe or anyone else your destination until after your first jump out of the system. Questions?"

"Are we leaving a major defensive hole at Brasilia, sir?" Carlos asked, still in wonder that he was about to have the heaviest possible thing he could imagine on his collar. A star.

"That's part of the secret with Yisan, Rear Admiral," Santos smiled now. "With a tentative agreement in place to stop as much of the hostile activity on that border as possible, we can withdraw some of those squadrons coreward."

"Which suddenly allows us to build up a significant reserve and possibly a fleet to go after Westphalia," Carlos nodded.

"Secondarily, yes," Santos agreed. "Right now, we need to hold Vilga, and the consensus is that you are right and Westphalia will attack to capture prisoners capable of giving them direct intelligence about Innruld coordinates. You will hold the system against them, Carlos. At all costs. *All* costs. If I have four months, I can reinforce you significantly, and even start going after Westphalia, instead of just trying to hold the wall against incursions. Buy me that time."

Santos rose now, so Carlos did as well. He accepted a firm handshake and tried to make sense of it all. He'd come in here to try and convince the man to do *something*.

When it turned out that *he* was the something.

"Where do I start, sir?" Carlos asked.

"Return to *Dutra* as a Captain," Santos said. "Brief Peláez and get her ready to fall in when you get the official orders to transfer to *Recife*. I've already started loading the squadron for a sail, and attached two cargo ships. Get everyone settled and then immediately depart, without any fanfare. I promise you one hell of a pinning party when you get back, but time and secrecy drive this."

"Understood, sir," Carlos said.

He found himself in the hallway fast enough, a copy of the signed promotion folded up and tucked into a jacket pocket right next to his heart.

How the hell had he gotten here? Except that they had picked him to haul Rod and Erlyn to Innruld Space. And Lazarus had sent him home escorting the most important colonists in Rio Alliance history.

And now he had to take command of a squadron and go protect the Churquen and Yithadreph on Vilga against Westphalia.

In his heart, suddenly-Rear Admiral Carlos Nguema knew that fuse was already burning.

THIRTY-SIX

ERLYN

ERLYN FOUND the exact moment when she lost her temper. Her hand slammed into the table top loud enough that everyone flinched. And Adriana Dunham woke up, which Erlyn truly regretted, but Roald needed to stop being a shit right now.

"Sorry," she whispered as Adriana popped up out of her carrier with a terrible squeak and Eha picked the little cutey up and coiled her around an arm and wrist, grabbing a bag of treats and popping one into a hungry mouth.

Erlyn took a deep breath and absolutely snarled at Roald. But silently. He had the courtesy to recoil a little.

"I don't really care what you think right now, Roald," she continued in a much quieter voice than before, honing all her angry emotion down from loud to a razor's edge that promised to start slicing pieces off the Chairman's hide soon.

"You overstepped, Erlyn," Roald growled back at her, also much quieter now that they had managed to wake the kit. "That was not your decision to make."

"Shall I move that we have a vote on the topic *right now*, Mr. Chairman?" Erlyn snapped, gesturing to the Council.

"Put all of you down on record with regards to supporting alien refugees who have come to us for help? I'm willing to push that hard if you feel like challenging me."

He saw that in her eyes. Roald Cavalcanti's hands came up placatingly, like he wasn't sure if he would win or lose such a vote, or how it would look to the people back home.

Quando no curso de eventos
Humanos…
When in the course of Human events…

"Erlyn, we don't need to be rash," Roald finally said, almost a whisper now.

She glowered across the table at him. Then the rest of the High Council, only skipping Eha with her wrath. They were all in the primary conference room, all equals around the table, with Eha and Adriana joining them for *discussions*. Which had been a code word for Roald Cavalcanti being an ass about things and threatening to tear up all the agreements that Oluchi had previously negotiated.

As Adriana finally munched contentedly, Eha leaned forward now, causing all nine heads to rotate her direction.

"Mr. Chairman, I'm already on record complaining that you have not allowed my deputy into this meeting," Eha said simply. "If you have decided that we need to start all of our negotiations over from scratch, I am happy to consider withdrawing entirely, where I will return to Vilga to have everyone pack up and depart from your colony world. We were originally planning to start on a place that was not as habitable as Liberty. I'm sure I could have a chat with Eduardo Martìnez or Fernanda Flores and they would be happy to relocate us, possibly to Yisan itself, or at least to a nearby world."

Even Erlyn felt the temperature of the room drop

precipitously at that threat. Because it wasn't a threat at all. It was a statement of purpose. Because Eduardo was here, now, on this planet, within immediate reach. And he would happily allow the Rio Alliance to cut its own throat and give up control over all trade with Innruld Space.

Erlyn had to remember that, as young as Eha was, she had been raised by Alla Dunham as a spy, and had run a significant network of agents in Innruld Space for more than a decade. That had included having people killed when they proved to be infiltrators.

Erlyn had finally met Alla in the flesh. Had spent a lot of time with the older woman who was currently acting as Governor of the Vilga colony, so Erlyn understood just how hard a person Eha could be. Would be, if pushed one millimeter further.

Pascia Nkali, the Gnashiiley Councilor who was nominally a member of the so-called Humanist Block on the Council and an adversary, leaned in and caught everyone's attention now. She was a quiet woman, most of the time, so you had to be quiet to hear her speak.

"I think that perhaps emotions have run a bit away with themselves," Pascia said in that solemn tone she did so well. "We are all intelligent beings and working towards a common goal, but occasionally things get excited and confused. I move that we recess for an early dinner now and perhaps not meet again as a High Council until tomorrow morning. Is there a second?"

Dead silence. It was a hell of a play, given the circumstances, but Pascia was no fool.

"Second," Erlyn spoke up when nobody else would.

Roald finally found his voice. Or maybe his balls, but Erlyn doubted that.

"It is moved and seconded," the Chairman spoke in a voice on autopilot. "All in favor? The motion carries."

He gaveled once, still quietly enough to not bother a kit, and everyone leaned back. Erlyn imagined that she could actually see steam coming off some of her fellow Councilors.

Eha was an elegant longsword carved out of emerald and honey. Or perhaps frozen nitrogen that had been brought down to a killing edge.

Erlyn rose and smiled at everyone. Like them, she needed to get out of this room before she probably said something she didn't necessarily regret later. Eha ended up just in front of her, with Adriana back in her bassinet, the little kit turned around to watch everyone, eyes bright and smiling as Erlyn made funny faces at her.

Erlyn's grandchildren were almost in their teens now, but kids and kits weren't all that different, she had found.

Pascia caught Erlyn's elbow with just a ghost of a pinch, but it was enough to nod her into a side chamber.

The space reminded Erlyn of a small chapel, emptied but still just large enough for the two chairs in here and a small table between them. Biped chairs. Erlyn had spent enough time around Churquen and even Yithadreph now, to appreciate something that simple.

They sat.

"This isn't exactly what we expected, when you went off exploring, Erlyn," Pascia began with a hint of a wry grin on her face.

"Agreed," Erlyn replied. "But circumstances forced my hand and, as you can see, Eha has options beyond Rio. We haven't exactly greeted her or the others with open arms. Plus, there is the treatment Lazarus has experienced."

"Lazarus," Pascia repeated the name. "I find it strange that so many people no longer call him Captain Oliveira, or even *Pancho*, according to my contacts. He has become *Lazarus of Bethany* in so many minds now."

"So history will record him, Pascia," Erlyn pointed out.

"His lucky accident has probably changed the future course of the galaxy."

"Agreed," the woman noted. "Before, the Rio Alliance was a Human-dominated place, run by Humans for the most part, although everyone reaped the benefits. But that's likely to change?"

"I doubt it," Erlyn turned to more fully face the woman now.

Pascia was younger, both in absolute years as well as relative to her expected lifespan. But still a canny operator.

"Why?"

"There are forty-some species in Innruld Space," Erlyn pointed out, "but if you brought over all of the Churquen, who are the largest group, they'd still be smaller than even the Moah for sheer numbers. And they won't reproduce that fast, at least for a century. Humans would stop being seventy percent of the population, assuming we absorb everyone in Innruld Space, but they'll still be the largest single group, as well as the fastest-growing."

"And if we managed to defeat Westphalia?" Pascia asked. "Somehow opened the entire galaxy up without those bastards having a say?"

"Eventually, I would expect Rio to either fragment some into regional elements, or to turn into some sort of grand empire that eventually broke down anyway," Erlyn said. "Human history is replete with examples, but none of those are likely to happen in our lifetimes. Our problems are much more compact and critical right now."

"Vilga," Pascia nodded.

"We have a colony of Churquen and Yithadreph, for the most part," Erlyn said. "There are others, but those two are ninety percent of everyone."

"The entire government structure of the Rio Alliance will have to change," Pascia nodded. "Certain structures were established early on to ensure that all aliens were given a voice and a seat at the table, so the Hall of Representatives will need to be recalculated soon. Even the High Council."

"I am not going to demand we rebuild the Council right now," Erlyn said flatly. "Eha and I talked and she is fine with being an Ambassadorial Representative for now. At least for a few years while we sort out Westphalia. Eventually, the government will need to change, at least as long as we succeed."

She watched Pascia relax.

"So what do you need in order to be happy with the situation, Pascia?" Erlyn asked, getting to the heart of why they were sitting here, alone with the door closed.

"Should we look at how the High Council is organized?" Pascia asked. "Even over a longer arc?"

"I would wonder if we didn't look to expanding it to eleven or maybe seventeen eventually," Erlyn replied. "Vilga will necessitate a change in representation out of balance with their current numbers, but they won't have as large an impact at lower levels, where things are by population or planet. Plus, there are Gnashiiley in Innruld Space, so eventually we might expect some of them to want to migrate here."

"Do we destroy the Innruld themselves?" Pascia asked. "Or seek to absorb them?"

From her tone, it was obvious that this was the question she really sought an answer to.

What to do with the so-called masters of the galaxy, who were not likely to be willing to cede power voluntarily.

"I'm not sure we could actually destroy them as a species, Pascia," Erlyn countered. "At least not until someone started offering bounties. Like Eha and Alla, they could just fill up a bunch of ships and flee into the darkness."

"Assuming they did, and I am, how long until they

rebuilt and became a threat?" Pascia asked now. "How soon do we face another Westphalia on a far flank?"

"Without Human technology, never," Erlyn replied. "I have been aboard the ships that brought the refugees to Vilga. Even the oldest, most broken down Human ship is better. More advanced. Plus, without technology, they are likely to revert even further, possibly to early industrial or worse before they managed to rebuild. Alla's people had spent a generation hiding machines to make tools, knowing that they would be on their own."

"Do we stop the Species Underground from hunting them?" the Gnashiiley Councilor asked, drilling in harder and harder.

Erlyn laughed out loud, unable to help herself. Pascia's snout crinkled in confusion.

"They are not—currently—part of the Rio Alliance, Pascia," she said around chortles. "So we don't get a vote. If they decide to formally join us later, then they are subject to our laws. Right now, I expect them to be a collection of what you might term country cousins on the back side of beyond. We can advise. We can offer trade, but unless they join us or we do the thing they fear and conquer them, they get to make those decisions."

Pascia leaned back now instead of answering. Erlyn finally relaxed.

At the end of the day, the two main voting blocks on the High Council really were just that. The Alliance Block, of which Erlyn was part, was happy to expand and locate new candidate species for Rio membership, assuming at the time that there had to be more than four sentient, tool-using species out there. The Humanist Block were more focused on holding Westphalia at bay, possibly even driving them back.

But everyone wanted to be free from those stifling shits on Earth and their opinions on how things should be done.

The silence stretched.

Finally Pascia leaned forward again and broke the yawning quiet.

"So if I tabled a motion to explore expanding the High Council to some greater number," she began carefully. "And we sent it to a committee with orders to report back in no more than a year…"

"I would support that, Pascia," Erlyn replied with a firm nod. "Might even make it two or three years, just to buy everyone time to adapt and understand that change is likely, but that we'll have a lot of time to talk about it first. After all, what else do we do but talk a lot?"

Pascia finally laughed. Smiled even. She held out a hand and Erlyn took it.

"Let's go see what we can do to ruin Roald's digestion," the woman suggested, rising.

Erlyn joined her, towering a little over the smaller woman, but only physically. In a few years, when Roald finally retired, Pascia Nkali might replace him as Chair. She was certainly capable enough.

They exited the chamber and Erlyn took a look at the hallways around her with new eyes.

What would Adriana Dunham's generation inherit?

THIRTY-SEVEN

OLUCHI

OLUCHI KNEW he was walking on a wire in a high wind, but the worst that could probably happen was a slap on the wrist and a stern talking to. On the one hand, he still had something like ambassadorial immunity. And he wasn't a Rio citizen. Seated beside him, Anya had a nervous smile pasted on her face.

Around them, the cargo shuttle slowly backed up and clunked against *Recife*'s hull. Lights came up from the dimness they had been running. Oluchi hadn't taken complete advantage of privacy and darkness to fool around all that much. About as far as one might go in a darkened cinema on a quiet afternoon. And Anya had started it.

"Sir, I'm going to just stay up on the cargo deck and pretend ignorance if asked," a man's voice came over the intercom.

"That's fine," Oluchi replied to the open air. "Thank you."

"Wouldn't have missed it."

"What?" Anya leaned close and whispered in his ear.

"Couple of fools thought they knew how to play poker,"

he turned and murmured into a cute ear as he kissed it. "When one doesn't have the money to call, you occasionally collect favors. That got us here."

"And if they throw a fit when they find us?" she asked.

Oluchi smiled and kissed her again. Just because.

"Then they might send us back to the ground," he shrugged, rising.

Around them, beeps and groans as the airlocks began to cycle.

He took Anya's hand and they both shouldered weekender bags. He was a civilian, down to the perfect opera cape. Oluchi would be damned before he was reduced to wearing borrowed military tan uniforms. Lazarus hadn't managed it. This new Rear Admiral on *Recife* wasn't about to.

The door opened and Oluchi planted them right in the way. A couple of sailors came into view and stopped dead with classical double takes.

"Are you supposed to be here?" the older of the two asked, checking against the clipboard he was carrying.

"No," Oluchi replied. "I need to talk to Admiral Nguema."

More double-takes. It was almost comical, in a way, watching, but he'd spent enough time around Rio sailors over the last year plus to understand how they were trained.

The older one nodded to the younger and pointed.

"Take these two to Lieutenant Sanchez and then return here immediately to help unload," he said. "You folks go with him and get out of my hair?"

"Gladly, Chief," Oluchi smiled and nodded.

The other sailor walked quickly, looking back just often enough to confirm that Oluchi and Anya had remained with him.

"Chief said to bring them to you, sir," the sailor said,

saluting and immediately departing, just to get out of the line of fire.

Lt. Sanchez's face turned confused, angry, and then sour just about that quickly.

"Stowaways?" Sanchez asked tiredly.

"Messengers for the Admiral," Oluchi lied convincingly.

It wasn't even all that much of a lie. Oluchi just hadn't mentioned who sent him. Or why. Of course, that required his entire rolodex to explain. He smiled instead.

"Marcos, haul them to the bridge," Sanchez said, turning to a handy sailor and gesturing over a shoulder.

Yup, Oluchi understood the bureaucracy. Convince everyone you meet that it's going to be easier to just send the problem on for someone else to deal with.

More corridors. More sailors looking at them in surprise as they went by, but not asking.

"How do you do that?" Anya whispered at one point.

Oluchi just smiled.

"Audacity and need," he explained. "It got me here. It will continue until it doesn't."

"You're nuts," she grinned.

"I will remind you that you seduced me, madame," he retorted with an equal smile.

"Under orders, Pryce," she laughed.

"Right," he laughed as well. "Orders."

Quickly, they ended up on the bridge. It was nothing like *Ajax*, but Oluchi wasn't surprised. Lazarus had explained how crowded they tended to be, with so many sailors packed in close to each other.

Marie Oslor happened to look up as they entered and for a moment he was afraid she was literally going to pass out from shock, but he winked at her and kept walking. Still, she locked her station and rose, moving to intercept them.

Marcos took that as a godsend.

"Lt. Sanchez said to bring them to the bridge, sir," he said nervously.

Marie studied the two of them closely for a long moment.

"I'll handle them, Marcos," she finally said.

Another sailor that left as if demons were on his tail.

"Dare I ask?" Marie glowered at the two of them.

Oluchi was feeling invulnerable.

"Need to talk to the Rear Admiral," he said. "Your old boss. What brings you to *Recife*?"

"I'm handling flag communications for the squadron," Marie replied. "Is Carlos going to order you thrown out an airlock?"

"Gods, I hope not," Anya spoke up. "This is all just a con job from the ground up."

Marie rolled her eyes and shook her head, but gestured them to follow her to a door off to one side, where she rapped, waited, and opened the door.

"Admiral, I know you'd rather not, but I have a situation you'll have to deal with eventually anyway," she said into the open hatch.

Oluchi and Anya were just enough off to one side that they couldn't see inside.

"Fine," Carlos's voice echoed tiredly. "Bring it."

Marie turned to them with a positively evil smile and ushered them in.

"Shit," Carlos said as soon as he saw them. "Marie, stay put for this."

Her face fell and it was Oluchi's turn to smile.

The four of them ended up in the admiral's office.

"Do I have a security leak I need to worry about?" Carlos asked, going back and forth across the three of them.

"No," Oluchi began. "Or rather, my spies are all on the civilian side. The Navy folk are a pain in the ass to turn."

"So how the hell did you end up on my deck, mister?" Carlos asked sourly.

"Sailors can't play poker for shit, Carlos," he replied, smiling to take the sting out of it. Most of the sting. "You know that."

"And?"

"And little birds whispered in my ear about a sudden promotion and transfer," Oluchi said. "Given *Recife*, I added two and two and liked the result. You are only a few hours from an unplanned departure, so I presumed that someone had finally listened to you and were sending a big enough hammer to Vilga to do the job."

Carlos sighed almost theatrically. One furred hand ran down from between his ears to the tip of his snout.

"Who else knows?" he finally asked.

"Eduardo sent me," Oluchi replied. "Eha as well, since I wear two hats. Currently, I'm asking to hitch a ride with you to Vilga so I can update Governors Garcia and Dunham, and start negotiating some deals for Yisan. Happy to bribe you and Marie with stock in a Limited Liability Corporation focusing on the Import/Export business. Sweat equity, as it were, for not sending me back to the surface on that same cargo shuttle."

Oluchi had only rarely seen a look on someone's face so acid that it might etch steel. Usually when the other guy knew that Oluchi had just drawn that fourth queen on the last hole card. But Carlos had it, in spades.

"When you are called to testify at my court martial," he began, "I expect you to tell them you held a pistol to my head."

"Happily, Carlos," Oluchi smiled and watched the other man relax.

"Marie, you will echo his testimony," Carlos turned to her.

Oluchi liked the young woman. She'd held her own with the others on the flight from Yisan to Vilga, so she was made of stern stuff.

"Assuredly, sir," she smiled.

Carlos looked them over again.

"If I leave you alone for a few hours, you think you can whip up some documents instructing me to haul you to Vilga as part of a diplomatic mission?" he asked. "They don't have to be particularly good forgeries, as long as I'm not lying when asked."

Oluchi laughed and pulled a bundle of papers from an inside pocket on his opera cape, handing them to Carlos across the desk.

"I can do worse, Carlos," he said. "These aren't forgeries."

"Of course not," Carlos sighed again. "Marie, find them quarters and make arrangements for the two ambassadors to join us in the officer's mess for meals."

He paused and studied them one last time.

"What do you expect to see at Vilga, Oluchi?" he asked in a voice betraying all the tiredness etched into his bones right now.

"The future history of the galaxy unfold, Carlos."

THIRTY-EIGHT

ADDISON

ADDISON REALLY, really, really wanted to bitch about it. Throw a screaming, twisting fit. Might have even indulged in a few histrionics in his cabin with the door closed.

But in the end he had acquiesced. *Force majeure*, which meant the same thing in Rio space as it did when shipping containers between Innruld stations.

Shit beyond my control.

So he stood coiled at attention as Rod da Silva approached, marching in a slow rhythm. Lazarus and Aileen stood to one side of Addison, with Kuei and Wybert beyond them. Ereshkiki Nisab, Thadrakho, Khyaa'sha, and Kemahle were on his other side, with both Cormac and Lenox in a second row in front of them.

It didn't help Addison's humor that everyone else was smiling.

Rod came to rest in front of him. Addison was leaning forward on his coil so the Admiral could reach out and remove the commander's tag he had been wearing semi-officially on his collar for the last however long, and replace it with the hollow circle of a Rio Alliance Naval Captain.

Him. Addison Wolcott. Churquen Director and occasional smuggler. Now a peer of Lazarus and Carlos. And however many more such men and women wore that heavy brass weight on their collar.

But he really had no choice, at the end of the day. Rod needed him. The Species Underground needed him.

The entire, stupid, freaking, greedy, lazy, never-to-be-sufficiently-damned galaxy needed him, when all Addison really wanted was to be home with his mate and their child.

Home. What a bizarre concept. His home had been *Shiva Zephyr Glaive* for more than a decade. At least when it wasn't *Ajax* or *Star of Kilri*.

Or this new command that he was about to assume responsibility for.

Grumble.

Rod finished fumbling with his collar and stepped back smartly, saluting with a smile on his face. Addison returned it, more or less adequately, even as his limbs and tail wanted to quake.

"Addison Wolcott, it is my distinct pleasure to promote you to the rank of Captain in the Rio Alliance Navy and enjoin upon you all the rights and responsibilities inherent in the duty," Rod said loud enough for everyone and the recording equipment to pick up. "Congratulations! All hands, dismissed."

And Addison found himself utterly engulfed in a hug by Lazarus, who got to him first. Aileen was close behind, which was weird, because hugs were mostly a Human thing, at least when you didn't have another Churquen to twine with.

Cheers and hands on his back and shoulder as everyone who had known him wanted to be engaged.

Addison gritted his teeth and accepted their jubilation. Even tried to enjoy it on their behalf. Rod and Lazarus had a special look in their eyes that Addison finally understood.

He had thought that being a Director of his own vessel, owner/operator, was a heavy load. All the risk. Only some of the reward, because you always had crew, fees, bribes, and bankers to deal with.

But that hollow ring on his collar weighed as much as *Shiva Zephyr Glaive*. At least those two men knew it, in ways that none of the others around him did.

Command of a warship, and everything that meant.

And he had to do it. Had to set an example for every member of Innruld Space that decided to join the Rio Alliance Navy one of these days and save the galaxy from the other Humans. And the Innruld.

Finally, the noise settled down. Some. People were still milling around. Most of them were old friends, but Briston Moora was a newcomer. Behind him, staying back along the wall of this large chamber, a whole row of what Addison wanted to think of as Elders, even though few of them were as old as he was, not counting the one Qooph who was probably two thousand years old from the way his rims looked. An older brother to Ereshkiki Nisab, as it were, even though they were probably not that closely related.

Addison fought his way through the mob of well-wishers and approached these folks. Glancing back, Lazarus and Rod had fallen in on his flanks, but stayed back even with his tail.

The leader of the group was a Tarni, another pinwheel spider like Khyaa'sha. Addison bowed to her carefully. Chera Sonels had reddish hairs almost down into orange. She was resting back on her abdomen and rear four legs so she could be upright and studying him.

He'd known Khyaa'sha long enough to see the gleam of a smile in her eyes.

"So what will you do now, Director/Captain Wolcott?" she asked in a dry, careful voice. "The Innruld will return soon enough."

Addison nodded. They would be. Losing a Pyramid and a station would be galling enough. To have Humans come along and frighten everyone would probably roust them to assemble a thing Lazarus had called an Armada.

But Addison had read enough naval history of Humans to understand that the original Armada had been an unorganized mob of fools trying to bluff their way through the superior sailing and fighting skills of the English. And they might have even succeeded, but for a storm.

How many times had an out-of-season storm altered the course of Human military history? England. Japan. Several others, where a calm day would have led to a probable conquest by forces that history recorded as evil. But history is the province of the winners, and Addison knew that.

But Sonels had asked him a question. A pointed one.

"We will recruit and train, madam," Addison replied. "Oton Mari Station will continue to be upgraded using Human technology and Human guns, just as this Pyramid will be. And make no mistake about it, Humans are far more advanced in fighting than the Innruld. They will come to us initially, but I have no doubts that Captain Lazarus and Admiral da Silva will take the war to them at some point."

"And the Species Underground?" she pressed. "What of us?"

"It is my hope that you will be able to hold Oton Mari," Addison said. "At the same time, if you send messages to other systems rousing them, we could use trusted sailors and workers to help build here. Right now, the only reason we don't go roll over every Security Pyramid in space is the lack of trained crew on all our vessels."

"Yes," she said sharply. "The Human War. Tell me, Humans, what will it mean when your kind invade our space?"

Addison glanced over at Lazarus, knowing that Rod

would defer to the man on such a question, even though he was senior. Rank only meant so much when you moved into political and cultural circles, and only Lazarus bridged both sides of the galaxy.

"It means that this station and this ship will be able to resist them," Lazarus replied calmly. "And as your people learn our technology, that you will be able to hold Innruld Space against Westphalia. They will come, eventually. Nothing the Innruld have can stop them. You can only blunt them for now, but the entire Species Underground will need to rise up for the Innruld to be cast down and this region of space become safe."

"And trade with your kind?" she asked, pivoting on her spinnerets to face Rod now.

"As soon as I can afford to send a ship home, I will invite it," Rod said, sternly erect as he bowed to her. "We are short-handed, as you know, and I cannot spare *Ajax* for any reason, but I hope that *Dutra* or another vessel will come."

"And I have already established banks in Human Space for you to call upon," Lazarus said. "For all the species to invoke, that they can secure cargoes at places like Yisan. It is only a beginning, but it is just that. A beginning between our two sides of the Nebula to form something new. Something free."

Addison rustled his scales to get her attention. Sonels turned back to him.

"With your help, the Innruld will fall, madam," he said. "It is as simple as that. Then you and Eha can sort out the future of everything else."

She nodded, but didn't seem convinced. But then, not many people had been paying attention when Cormac blew the top of this Pyramid off with one well-placed shot from a Star Spear. And they were mounting Star Lances now, both here and at Oton Mari.

"There is a storm coming," Lazarus interjected. "But I intend to prevail."

Addison shivered to the tip of his tail, thinking back to that conversation with Cormac and wondering.

Would Addison Wolcott end up being the voice of reason? Or vengeance?

THIRTY-NINE
LAZARUS

LAZARUS LOOKED around *Ajax*'s bridge with a hard smile. Addison's Pyramid was finally functional again and upgraded enough to defend local space against all comers. There were hundreds of other Security Pyramids out there, but the Innruld wouldn't dare leave that many systems to their own devices for long enough to assemble a true fleet.

What they would likely do, once they heard about an alien ship that had taken that first Pyramid by surprise, would be to send four or maybe as many as six to overawe the locals, expecting that they would have sufficient firepower to deal with any intruder.

Lazarus grinned to himself as he looked along the line of his bridge, so extended like a goose's neck because of Kirov's Lance. How many would they send? How many could he destroy?

How much terror and chaos could *Ajax* sew among those tall bastards?

He knew it was wrong to be looking forward to such a thing, but Innruld Space was still just a stepping stone on his way to Westphalia and Earth. Somehow, it had fallen onto his shoulders to save the galaxy, although he could hardly think of a stranger outcome.

He had only intended to go down with his ship.

The admiral's hatch opened and Rod emerged slightly onto the bridge to wave Lazarus to join him. Could have just called on the intercom, but Lazarus guessed that they were all getting a little stir crazy.

Lazarus left Kuei in charge and took the chair, studying Rod da Silva. The man looked more tired and yet more alive than Lazarus remembered.

"How is the crew holding up?" Rod asked as they settled.

"Running hard, but that's nothing new," Lazarus said. "With as many people as I could spare over on the Pyramid and the station, we're almost back to the skeleton crew I had when I went to Yisan."

"Can we still fight when the Innruld arrive?" Rod asked.

"Easily," Lazarus nodded. "They have nothing to resist Kirov and no clue that the only way to overwhelm us right now would involve swarms of little gunships, since Wybert would be firing everything manually from the bridge. Pyramids are just that much dead meat. Why?"

"We've sent all the Innruld and their troops home," Rod said. "That starts a clock ticking, but nobody knows how organized they are to respond. I'm lost, because I'm used to dealing with organized navies, and Innruld is anything but."

"And we can't really scout that much," Lazarus agreed. "I mean we can, as long as we go point to point between here and close systems, but they use trans-space, so they could just emerge here after we left."

"I know," Rod groused. "Considered ordering Enjehn to take *Star of Kilri* and scout, but at the end of the day, that's a half dozen people I need here getting ready. How soon will we have a trained-up crew on the Pyramid that we could take it somewhere?"

Lazarus leaned back and considered the question. The Species Underground were moving, but he'd asked them all to come out into the open finally, and not everyone had been willing. Even when Addison had asked.

The Pyramid required a crew of nearly a thousand, but could get by with only a few hundred, since Addison didn't need torturers or even prison guards. And Cormac could run larger chunks of the vessel better than even a team of people.

"We're thin, Rod, simple as that," Lazarus finally answered. "The messages have gone out, but I expect that every ship that normally frequents Oton Mari is going to be subject to a lot of hassling by the Innruld, once the masters of the galaxy hear about this. A few ships will just disappear off their regular routes and show up here, but they are not prepared for active rebellion."

"If I could just go blow some things up, it would be better," Rod said. "Get people's attention. But like you said, we're stuck here until they can start outfitting a force with Star Spears and Star Lances that can defend Oton Mari."

"Training is moving forward," Lazarus at least had a small reason to smile. "This is a mining station, so you have a lot of spacers. Downside, they tend to be wildly independent owner/operators most of the time, so they don't have a lot of interest in military discipline. I expect that will change once we fight a big battle here and win."

Rod nodded. Lazarus could see the stress. Everything he did was going to be judged by the High Council when they all got home, and Erlyn Teixeira wasn't around to offer advice.

Pedro Santos would be responsible for all their fates. Well, everyone else. Lazarus would be willing to stay here and never return to Rio space again. Grace would probably remain behind with him, if he asked.

Let everyone else fall on their swords for a bunch of short-sighted bureaucrats on Brasilia.

"We will win," Lazarus continued. "They have nothing to stand against us."

"That part I'm not worried about, Lazarus," Rod said.

"What then?"

"Westphalia somehow making common cause with the Innruld," Rod said. "At least for a little while. Overcoming their cultural chauvinism long enough to stretch the Rio Alliance too far and then swoop in on us from two sides."

"Do you send Aileen home for orders and updates?" Lazarus asked. "*Star of Kilri* would be able to make that run, however slow, if she had an engineer who could repair everything that broke. That maybe convinces the fleet to throw some more people here. We don't even need hulls. Just bodies."

"I will think on it," Rod said. "Thank you."

Lazarus recognized a dismissal and rose. There should be news soon. Carlos Nguema had the coordinates for Oton Mari, and knew what they were up to.

What had happened back home to prevent him from returning?

CARLOS LOOKED over *Recife's* thronged bridge. Much bigger than *Dutra's*. Even more crowded.

And that was before he added Pryce and Persaud to the mix. Vilga wasn't that far away, thankfully.

Still, Carlos grumbled.

"What was that?" Oluchi asked. "I caught something about genies and wishes."

Carlos scowled at him. At least he wasn't stupid enough to play poker with man. Anya had warned several people. As had Marie Oslor.

"Poisoned chalices, Pryce," Carlos said. "You get the thing you wished for, but it rarely turns out right."

"You're doing fine, Carlos," Oluchi dropped his voice. "I watched Lazarus do this and he had a much rougher time, because he was working with civilian aliens. You've just got a couple of hitchhikers along."

"And the possibility of yet another major fleet action at Vilga's Stand, this time with the added attraction of civilians on the ground that I need to protect."

"So I've read up on the battle Lazarus and *Ajax* fought

most recently," Anya stepped in. "At least as much as the civilians were allowed to know, but Erlyn gave me a copy. How does *Recife* stack up against a ship like *Gotland?*"

"Comparable across the board," Carlos said. "Heavy Starcruisers, both of us. They do a little better with big guns because of the expectation of a GunWall in between. We do better with medium firepower for the same reason."

"How soon until someone replicates Kirov's Lance and puts it on a ship?" Oluchi asked, thinking back to that deadly swan that had carried him from Yisan to Brasilia. Everything since had been something of a letdown, being more boxy and less elegant.

Carlos scratched at the fur on the right side of his chin.

"They didn't know that it worked until *Gotland,*" he replied, trying to frame things in civilian terms without giving away too much. Rod da Silva had brought him deeper into the situation than Carlos's security clearance might otherwise have justified. "From there, they might decide to steal the plans if they can, or reverse engineer it. Either way, couple of years before they could even start to lay a hull. I'm guessing without being told that Fleet would have already started building another *Ajax*, but Lazarus didn't stay around to answer a lot of technical questions and his reports were apparently a little vague in places. Possibly intentionally."

"So traditional warships going at each other?" Oluchi clarified.

"Yes, with us having the advantage of a defensive station in orbit, as well as the ball and chain around our ankle from it," Carlos nodded. "Hard nut to crack, but we can't chase them all that well, unless we get some lucky shots home. But I don't have to do more than hold the field."

"So will you keep *Dutra* here or send it on to help Admiral da Silva?" Oluchi asked.

"More poisoned chalice decisions," Carlos replied. "If I

keep them, that's a few extra guns at a time when that might make the difference? If I send them on, does that give da Silva the edge he needs to finish off the Innruld? None of us can be everywhere, and the lag on messages can be months."

"Is there anything we can do?" Oluchi asked.

"Wanna take an old Churquen freighter and try to navigate it all the way to Oton Mari?" Carlos grinned at the two of them.

"Would it help?" Oluchi asked, suddenly alert in a most helpful manner that had Carlos's guard up.

He studied the Human. Both Humans, as they had suddenly changed their demeanor significantly.

"What's your game?" Carlos asked.

"Part of why I'm here is to help facilitate communications, Carlos," the man said. "Eha and Eduardo have both sent message packs along, with the expectation that I will be working on things at Vilga. At the same time, trade between the two nations is where I intend to get rich."

"So I might be playing directly into your hands by sending you over?" Carlos asked.

"It will be to everyone's benefit in the long term," Oluchi replied.

"Fine," he said. "If you can find a crew willing to haul you back, I'll put you in command of the boat and let you turn into a pirate."

"Not much piracy, if the ship is an unarmed, Innruld eggshell," Anya observed.

"You can't have one of my warships," Carlos laughed.

"No, but what if I was able to pull a swindle on the captain of *Celestial Sovereign*?" Oluchi asked.

"Eduardo Martìnez's yacht?" Carlos asked. "What's the difference then?"

"It's rather heavily armed," Oluchi smiled. "Perhaps not

sufficient to engage a GunWall, but probably far more than any equivalent Innruld vessel."

Carlos fell silent. He hadn't given thought to that yacht. But if it was armed like a Yisan oligarch might choose, then it would probably be hell on wheels over there.

"You convince the captain and I'll let you do it," Carlos said. "We'll need to send a raft of signals over if you can, but that will help. Plus, I might be able to thin out my crews a little to send you some people. I can't imagine Rod and Lazarus wouldn't need trained sailors, whatever they've been up to."

He watched the two Humans nod excitedly and excuse themselves, which was the best part. It got them out of his fur at a time when he needed to be working with this new crew and new squadron.

But he couldn't help wondering if he'd just been swindled. Again.

FORTY-ONE

AILEEN

AILEEN WASN'T ENTIRELY happy with it, but in the end she didn't have a tailstub to balance on with this one. Briston Moora had trained as a mechanic, which was close enough to an engineer for her needs. *Star of Kilri* had been through a solid enough refurb at the hands of excellent Rio engineers, as well as Ereshkiki Nisab, that she trusted it. And he had been minding his manners around her sufficiently that she didn't think he'd be a problem when it was just the two of them alone.

Plus, Xiuying's lessons on close combat were still fresh, if she ended up pretending to be a Human in fur. But she didn't say that to the kid. Too easy to frighten him, when he was already a little intimidated by her.

Like she preferred.

"Engineering, are we ready for trans-space flight?" she said into the intercom, looking around the completely empty bridge.

Didn't need a lot of crew. The ship was intended to be flown by two, with the others cooking, cleaning, commanding, and shooting guns.

"I think so," Briston answered.

"Think or know, sailor?" she barked at him, sounding just like Lazarus in her head.

"Everything is green, Director," Briston replied this time.

"Good enough," Aileen said to the universe.

She was seated in the pilot's chair, rather than the command throne, but that was just a personal preference, as both could fly the ship.

Star of Kilri vanished from the universe and entered the pearl-colored corridor of trans-space. She'd done the math with Kuei's help and determined that it was faster to go through the Nebula, even with the twists and turns, than to go over or under. *Ajax* could do those, as could any Rio or Westphalian ship with jump drives, but she was stuck sailing the slow way. At least she could turn.

Aileen sat for a few minutes to make sure everything was behaving, and then set the autopilot to cover things and warn her if it had any problems. She unbuckled and rose, heading aft to find Briston standing at the main console muttering to himself as she stood in the doorway.

Nothing like a crash course in a whole bunch of engineering fields, but Addison had needed Ereshkiki Nisab and Thadrakho to keep the Pyramid from breaking down, and Lazarus barely had enough people left to fly *Ajax*, not that he was going anywhere for a while.

Briston looked over at her with a start and a gasp.

"Sorry," he said.

"It's okay," Aileen grinned. "Snuck up on you."

"You do that," he muttered ambiguously.

Aileen considered bantering with him, but decided that the kid was still a little too nervous, so she just walked in and found a spot to sit, out of his way, where she could watch him work.

She liked to tease him as a kid, but he was an adult, just a decade younger than her. Unseasoned, maybe, when she'd gotten a little too jaded out in the big, bad universe as a criminal and smuggler.

And she was in charge here by command of the alien admiral, which hadn't helped the kid stay on balance.

"What's Human Space like?" Briston finally asked as he worked, head still down and fingers deftly adjusting knobs and sliders as he listened to the ship fly.

"Outsized," Aileen replied. "Remember, you're dealing with folks who do things to Innruld scale, but they are way more violent. And stronger. They'll outnumber us whatever to one, except when we get to wherever Eha and Alla finally landed the colonists."

"Are they all like Lazarus?"

"More are than aren't, from what I saw when I was there," Aileen said, letting her voice turn dark. "But Westphalia is different, and there will be people who hate you because you aren't Human. Nothing more. I got beaten pretty badly by a group of folks on Yisan who worked for a man like that."

"What did you do?" Briston asked.

"Watched Lazarus, Grace, and a few others kill all of them," Aileen said. "Lazarus kicked open the door and Xiuying literally shot everyone in the room except the guy holding a gun to Eha's head."

"Eha Dunham, the Churquen, right?" he said.

"Correct," Aileen nodded. "Addison's mate. You'll meet her when we reach the far end of this trip."

"I'm not sure I'm the one that they should have sent," he finally said after a few moments of silence. "You probably need an expert engineer, and I'm kinda a generalist."

"They needed all trained hands back at Oton Mari," Aileen replied. "Plus, this ship got rebuilt enough that we should be good. Once we get there, we can ask someone in

Rio space to either send some engineers back with us, or give us a bigger ship and crew. You'll do fine."

In her head, Aileen had to stifle the giggles. This conversation was almost identical to the one she'd had with Lazarus and da Silva when they had approached her to fly to Rio space to get more help.

But this was what it meant to be Second Officer on *Ajax*. Like when da Silva had sent Marie Oslor and the others off from *Dutra* to Yisan with the captured Westphalian Scout Wall.

You did things because you were the person best suited and available when the need arose.

"How's everything doing back here?" Aileen continued when Briston just sat and watched her.

"I think it's all doing pretty good," he shrugged. "Everything is on the beam right now and all the variances are within tolerances. It's when we start seeing other issues or things breaking down that I'll have to freelance."

"Which is why they sent you and not someone else," Aileen smiled. "I needed a redneck like Lazarus who could just come up with something, rather than panicking because we didn't have the exact right part in stock."

"The Director is a redneck?" Briston gasped. "But he's a scientist."

"That's a cover, kid," Aileen laughed. "Him and Thadrakho used to nerd out over the weirdest technical things, back when we were just smugglers on *Shiva Zephyr Glaive*. He might have designed and built *Ajax*, but he's just like you underneath it all."

"Huh," he blinked, watching her.

Aileen watched something change in his eyes. A newfound confidence took root. That was good. Something would break. Something always broke.

But the kid would be much more ready to fix it.

"I'm going forward to make myself some tea," she announced. "Get you anything?"

"Yeah, that would be nice," he replied. "Want to watch things here for a bit. Got a few temperature readings that concern me. Wondering if I have a leak somewhere I need to tape before it gets big."

Aileen nodded now and headed out. They'd get there.

And maybe have a different conversation one of these days.

FORTY-TWO
OLUCHI

OLUCHI STUDIED THE WOMAN, certain that his gambit was going to fail. Antonia Veracruz, captain of Eduardo's yacht, *Celestial Sovereign*. She was a tiny woman, physically. Barely five feet tall and slender to the point of petite. Early fifties, where her hair had turned completely gray now on the way to white, but she didn't seem to care, wearing it shoulder length and showing off the waves of color as it faded, from darkness at the tips to white at her skull.

She had a noncommittal look on her face even now, having listened to his spiel.

They were on her bridge, aboard *Celestial Sovereign*: him, Anya, Captain Veracruz, and a few crew members apparently pretending to be deaf and invisible. The air was even still.

"Eduardo could have sent you with orders to go to Innruld Space, Pryce," she finally said.

It wasn't a firm no, but it also wasn't an enthusiastic yes.

"This came up after we departed Brasilia, Antonia," he replied. "We were going to Vilga to negotiate some new deals with Alla Dunham. Carlos needs someone to make the long run to Lazarus. He can't send any of his ships because he'll need them here if Westphalia attacks. I would think that Eduardo would want you to know the sailing directions, as well as start making personal connections with folks over there, so he can start sending freighters, once Lazarus clears the way."

"And if we get attacked by Innruld ships or pirates?" she asked.

Anya laughed out loud before Oluchi could reply.

"You think anything less than a Security Pyramid is a threat to this ship?" she asked. "Even that might be iffy. I've seen some of your specs, Captain."

Oluchi liked the way Antonia's face darkened with a blush.

"What's your game, Pryce?" she finally asked.

"I want to get rich, Antonia," he replied now. "At the same time, I've always been the playboy diplomat. When Eha and Lazarus went off to Vilga the first time, they left me behind to keep lines of communication open. Now, I'm almost doing the same thing, but Carlos suggested I take one of the colonist's ships. I would like to use *Celestial Sovereign* because maybe for once I can do something other than seduce pretty women and run errands for more important people."

He didn't like the way his own face got a little hot as he spoke, or how his voice sounded, but two years ago he had been a gigolo on Yisan, facing the end of his useful career and wondering if he would have to transition to con man to make a living.

Then Eha and Aileen had arrived.

"So you don't plan on seducing me, Pryce?" Antonia asked, eyeing both him and Anya in a peculiar manner.

Oluchi nearly took the bait, but something stopped him.

"You know what, Antonia?" he asked, voice suddenly calm and flat. "No. I've asked you to reinterpret your orders from Eduardo in a new manner. You'll choose to do so, or not. If not, I'll find some other vessel to haul me to where Lazarus is and that will be the end of it. Good enough?"

Her eyes got a little big and shocked for a moment. Probably still remembered the gigolo, and hadn't been expecting him to call her bluff like that.

Tough, lady. People change. Maybe even grow up.

But he didn't say that to her. Just focused a hard look on the woman, daring her to guess wrong.

Apparently, she could move quickly when she wanted to, however. Antonia Veracruz stood up a little straighter.

"So does this make us a military vessel, Pryce?" she asked, skipping right over all the boring, fiddly bits in between.

"I do not have that authority, Captain Veracruz," he replied. "I can, however, ask Governor Dunham to issues you *Letters of Marque and Reprisal.* Won't count for much, other than provide some legal fig leaf if the Rio High Councilors get their noses out of shape. We'd still be pirates."

"That's nothing new," Antonia smiled. "You talk to your people and find out what staff the admiral wants to send along while I get the ship resupplied for a long haul. I presume the admiral will be willing to stock us up."

"That he will," Oluchi said.

Quickly, he and Anya found themselves in a shuttle heading to the ground for the next part of his little table game. Anya turned to study him closely.

"You could have seduced her, you know," she observed quietly, even though they were the only two back in the personnel bay. "She would have gone along with it."

"I don't want to be *him* anymore, Anya," Oluchi replied, maybe a little stiffly. "I want to be someone people respect, not pity. I want you to look at me as a partner, not a thinly-veiled con man selling a pig in a poke. I wasn't bluffing about taking one of the shit freighters on the ground if she'd have said no."

"And she realized that pretty quickly," Anya agreed, leaning in to kiss him on the cheek. "I know who you are. The others are only now figuring that part out."

He turned and kissed her back, thinking that they had a while before they got to the ground. Maybe he needed to show this wonderful woman just how much he appreciated her. Things were going to get a little weird soon.

Or perhaps a lot.

FORTY-THREE

EHA

EHA STUDIED the three High Councilors that had called upon her today, wondering what game they were about now. Roald Cavalcanti, Erlyn Teixeira, and Pascia Nkali.

Erlyn she counted as a friend. The other two were politicians, simple as that.

They were all in a front room in the suite Eha had been assigned. Ambassadorial, and all that, but she didn't have a staff of any kind, with Oluchi and Anya off to Vilga. Adriana was asleep in a Human crib, a small cage made out of wires, roughly three feet on a side and about a foot and a half tall. It would not hold a curious Churquen who could already climb, but it would give her a place to rest.

Tea had been served. Eha had tried coffee once, to be polite. She preferred tea.

She focused now on the other three, but mostly on Cavalcanti.

He took a deep breath and sucked his lips inward for a moment before speaking.

"As we always expected it would, news of alien contact has finally gotten out to the general public," he began slowly.

Eha arched a set of eye scales at the man and cocked her head just so. It wasn't a Churquen body language thing, but she'd seen Lazarus and Erlyn do it enough times that she had learned the trick. Semi-sarcastic inquiry, without actually committing words. She would have spiraled the last two feet of her tail instead. Or rather, in addition.

"Journalists are clamoring for more information," he continued. "As well as personal interviews."

Eha allowed herself a tiny smile. No doubt Oluchi and Anya, possibly with the approval and maybe assistance of Erlyn, had leaked things that had flowed outward like ripples.

"I see," she replied diplomatically, not letting them have any scales to catch on.

"We would like to invite two such journalists here to interview you at some point," he continued. "Understanding that certain things to be agreed on beforehand won't be discussed due to military sensitivities."

"Obviously," she noted.

"What he's dancing around, Eha, is the question of how much damage you would intend to do, given such a platform," Pascia said now, grinning at Roald's discomfort.

Eha nodded to the woman. And shared her smile.

"It is not in my interest to damage the Rio Alliance, Pascia," Eha replied, turning to the woman. "Our goal has always been to find a place that we could escape the Innruld and build a new life. Free. If anything, we'd be more interested in how we could help you punch Westphalia in the snout, because without them, all the species could sail anywhere they wanted and start new lives. Does that help?"

"Would you be willing to be part of a patriotic drive?" Erlyn spoke up now.

"Patriotic?" Eha asked.

"New temporary taxes, perhaps war bonds. That sort of thing," Erlyn offered. "We need money if we wish to build up our fleet to the point that we could consider fighting a two-front war effectively."

"Ah, but my people are currently just refugees, according to Rio legal standards," Eha countered, focusing now on Roald Cavalcanti. "We intend to petition to join the Alliance, but have not done so. I appreciate that such a move on my part to assist your ship-building and recruiting might bear fruit long term, but there are other considerations."

As in, what's in it for me? For Adriana? For my people on Vilga and the others that Lazarus and Addison are even now working to liberate?

Erlyn and Pascia both shared her serene smile, so perhaps they had already had such a discussion with Roald before this and not been able to move the man. The High Council contained a Humanist Block as well as an Alliance Block, but all those old calculations were being tilted now.

"That is a trade we are willing to discuss, Ambassador," Chairman Cavalcanti said now. "We have been sending resources to Vilga as well as to Innruld Space, and now it begins to appear that the war with both enemies is moving to a higher tempo, to quote Admiral Santos. We need to look beyond mere liberation of the various species from Innruld control, and move on to a grand alliance that will hopefully be sufficient to break Westphalia entirely as a power."

"You will never convince some people that they should welcome strangers of other colors and shapes," Pascia interjected, basically agreeing with the man. "But without an official imprimatur, they become shrill voices in the wilderness that can be ignored until they take some sort of illegal action, and then actively suppressed."

Eha disliked the thought that such opinions could just be

shut down. She had lived her entire life until now under a similar Innruld threat. What could the galaxy be like without the Innruld or Westphalia threatening everyone? But there would always be a few. Best if they could be contained.

She smiled and nodded.

FORTY-FOUR

AILEEN

AILEEN STUDIED the various charts and sensor readings, just to be sure. This had all been second nature to Kuei, but Aileen had been a Loadmaster, not a pilot. She was a long ways from home, but everything looked right.

Don't come out too close, but not too far away either. Just right to slip back into trans-space if necessary.

"Briston, we're thirty seconds out," she called on the intercom. "Stand by for real space."

They'd only lost a half-day so far, as long a sail as this had been. And even that had merely been a coolant line blowing out and necessitating replacement and a lot of tape to hold things in place. Hopefully, she could sell off this hunk of junk to a scientist who wanted to understand Innruld technology better, and end up with a Rio-grade ship. Maybe the fleet had a budget?

The freighter dropped out of trans-space and Aileen pinged everyone and everything hard, identifying herself and praying that the ships answering would be Rio. She was well above the ecliptic of the system and out a ways from the planet where the Dunhams intended to land their colony, and anything might have happened.

Lots of ships around her, but they all had Rio transponders, so she dared hope. Then a blueshift went off right next to her.

Damn, someone's on the ball and twitchy to move that fast.

"Unknown vessel, this is Protector/Leader Three Seven One," a man's voice came over the standard frequency. "Identify yourself."

"*PL-371*, is Commander Rodriguez still aboard?" Aileen asked. "If so, this is Commander Aileen Enjehn aboard a captured Innruld vessel with updates and orders from Admiral da Silva."

There. Even sounded like a professional sailor. All those hours taking correspondence courses weren't probably wasted.

"Roger that, Commander," he replied. "We'll come alongside shortly on a shuttle to inspect you."

"Standing by, *371*," Aileen said.

She reached out and cut all the engines now, letting the sluggard drift and not threatening everything. If the protector squadron was still around, that was a good sign. She looked at her boards again and realized that the flagship over there was *Recife*, which was a little jarring. Who would they have promoted to command that squadron and this whole system, if Rod da Silva was still at Oton Mari?

"Briston, we're shut down," she relayed aft. "There will be Human marines coming aboard in a little while to inspect everything, and then the ship will probably be confiscated, so make sure you have all your stuff packed up."

"Confiscated, Aileen?" Briston replied.

"I don't want to keep it, kid," she laughed. "We're probably going aboard the flagship from here. The only question is if they have us leave the ship in orbit or land it with the others. Probably the former, but I don't plan on coming back unless I have to."

"Gotcha."

She made her way midship and got the last of the fresh juice before she had to defrost more. Had that and a snack as the ship sensors pinged quietly with collision warnings that she ignored. The machines were too stupid to understand that they were about to be boarded, and she didn't have Cormac to override everything and keep them quiet.

Briston came forward with a bag slung over his shoulder. He saw what she was up to and raided the fridge as well.

"So what's next?" he asked.

"Well, if you want to be a sailor, they'll enlist you and start training you immediately," she said. "I'm an officer until they finally change their minds and let me quit, so I'll be talking to whatever admiral they put in charge."

"What else could I do?" he asked tentatively.

They'd had this discussion before, but it had all been theoretical then. Time to load cargo now, bucko.

"You could join the colony on the surface," Aileen opined. "There are a number of Yithadreph with them, those and Churquen being the two largest groups, so you'll have people to talk to. At some point, they may send a ship to Innruld Space, so you'd have the option to return there if you really wanted, but likely you'd be a sailor on a warship at that point, as there won't be anyone hauling cargo for a while."

"Is it okay if I want to stick close to you?" he asked, whiskers and ears flat backwards at his embarrassed audacity.

Aileen smiled. She'd been hoping he might say something like that, but had intimidated the kid from the beginning. To this point, she hadn't even asked him to scrub her back in the shower. Kid might have died of fright had she suggested it.

"We'll see what we can do," she assured him.

The hull began to ring, so she rose and walked to the airlock in time to hear it beeping as it opened.

Six Humans in spacer armor and guns entered, professionally dangerous and a little too high-strung for her tastes.

Aileen saluted the closest one with her cup of juice and went back to drinking it as the others swarmed the place, sticking noses and guns in the few rooms while two of them kept guns pointed at her and the kid. Briston did a pretty good job of nonchalance, munching on a bag of nuts. If you didn't know Yithadreph body language, it might even be convincing.

"Sir, our instructions were to leave this ship stable with nav beacons on," the closest marine finally said. "We are to transport you and your crew to Admiral Nguema aboard *Recife* soonest."

Nguema? Former captain of *Dutra*? Wow. Things had gotten weird.

"I need three minutes to grab my gear," Aileen replied. "Ship is currently running okay, but you'll want to shut it completely down or find somewhere to land it in a day or three."

"Understood."

And quickly enough she found herself and the kid flying aboard a shuttle. Quick blueshift dropped them at the flagship and they landed. Briston's eyes were huge, but he had a pretty good view out the front window as they flew, and *Recife* was a damned impressive ship.

All the usual rigmarole for a Commander coming aboard, but they skipped most of it and got her and Briston to Admiral Nguema pretty quickly. Same guy, more rank.

Maybe more smiles, but *Dutra* had been a tub, little better than the one she'd been flying to get here, so this was a big promotion.

He surprised her with a hug instead of a salute. It was a Human thing, and neither of them were, but it was also touch, in a place where sailors and marines were too busy out-toughing each other.

He hugged Briston as well, a Gnashiiley engulfing a shocked Yithadreph, and then everyone got sat down. Most of the others in the room were Human, and the only one Aileen recognized was Marie Oslor.

But the Rio fleet had taken it seriously enough.

"Talk to me," Carlos ordered in a friendly voice.

FORTY-FIVE

CARLOS

ADMIRAL *CARLOS NGUEMA. Can't forget the ramifications of the title.*

He was more than just captain of *Dutra* now. His responsibilities included an entire solar system, an armed station, a colony of nearly a dozen sentient species, and a small fleet of scouts, gunships, and various Starcruisers. Enough to weigh on the soul.

He'd met Enjehn in Innruld Space with da Silva. Second Officer on *Ajax*, and now messenger from the other side of the galaxy with news as he listened to her finish her tale of events around Oton Mari. He would have given nearly anything to be able to have gone with a rescue force. Or even sent one, but he needed every vessel he had here, now, against the attack he was expecting from Westphalia.

And he was expecting it soon.

Technically, three days ago, given the best possible flight times from information to make that leap, coalesce on the other side in the form of a force to come here, and then arrive.

"Thank you, Commander," he said as Aileen finished and looked around the room.

Captain Quispe, the actual commander of *Recife*, had dealt with her before, as had several others on this ship. Carlos had brought Marie with him from *Dutra* to handle communications, and to groom her for her own command one of these days. Certainly, she'd earned several gold and silver stars next to her name since everything that had happened in Innruld Space.

Carlos studied the group. There were more around the edges of the room, but he would make decisions. The rest were here to answer questions.

"Paulo, her ship isn't worth anything but study, according to what I heard, so maybe we leave it in place for now and eventually haul it to Brasilia for the boffins to rip apart, unless you need it now?" Carlos asked.

"Faster using a pincke to do anything, Carlos," the Captain of *Recife* replied with a grin.

"Aileen, did you have subsequent orders, after arriving here?" he asked.

"Mostly to convince the fleet to protect the colony, if they hadn't already moved to do so," she replied with a nod in his direction.

"Can I assign you to the colonial government as a Quartermaster for a while, then?" he pressed, knowing that he could order it, but that she wasn't nearly as committed to military order as most of the people in the room. "Alla Dunham doesn't really understand our systems, so you could go a long ways towards smoothing things out and making sure we deliver the right supplies for the colonists."

And, you wouldn't have to serve aboard a warship. Lazarus let me know that most of his old comrades weren't warriors, not counting Wybert.

Aileen did smile now.

"That would be lovely, Admiral," she said. "Second best option to returning to *Ajax*, but we can arrange something soon enough."

Carlos liked the subtle threat that she wouldn't be afraid to kick at his authority, but he'd seen her work over there, and Lazarus trusted her more than anyone else. Good thing to keep in mind.

Carlos started to speak when a chime overrode everything in the room.

"Admiral, we have an alert," a female voice come over the line.

He didn't recognize her, but he was still adjusting to the huge crew and meeting everyone. He'd get there, but not today.

"Status?" he barked, everyone in uniform automatically rising now, which did not include the two Yithadreph, not that he was surprised.

"One of our scouts just checked in with news of a force of enemy warships gathering at one of the suspected checkpoints, Admiral," she said emphatically.

"All ships to battlestations and begin maneuvering to avoid ambush," he called. "This meeting is done. Aileen, you and your assistant stand by and I'll see if we can get you to the surface right now before all hell breaks loose."

She paused and he watched her whiskers and ears work over some problem.

"If it was all the same, sir, we'll stay here for now," she said, falling in with him as well as the two of them could with short legs.

Carlos was used to keeping up with Humans, but he slowed now to let his crew outdistance him.

"How about I put you on the flag bridge with me," he offered. "Marie will handle communications with the fleet, but you can keep Alla up to date. There's not much her folks can do, but at least she can know."

"What happens if they drive you off, Admiral?" she asked now.

"I'll be dead by then, Commander," he explained. "The only way they'll get to her is through the bodies of me and all my crews."

"Oh."

Carlos nodded and began to jog. She kept up.

Westphalia wasn't going to treat new aliens any better than they did the ones they already had. Maybe worse.

But that was why Admiral Santos had sent him here. And why Rod and Lazarus had trusted him with all those lives.

FORTY-SIX

AILEEN AND BRISTON ended up with Marie Oslor down on the flag bridge, not all that far from Admiral Nguema. At the last battle for Vilga, she had been all the way aft, doing an inventory of supplies, since the kitchens had been shut down.

She wondered if those same rules would hold here. The Rio Alliance Navy had lots of snack food packs that you just opened and ate directly, without needing to heat or cool, so it wasn't like anyone would go hungry while they waited. Same for energy drinks in weird aluminum cans.

Thankfully, she didn't have to organize things for this crew. *Recife* probably had four times the crew that *Ajax* had been designed for, but Lazarus had intentionally automated as much as possible and had fewer guns requiring crews.

By the time everything was organized, Aileen found herself sitting next to Lt. Oslor, with Briston on her far side. He didn't have anything to do, so she echoed a few different boards onto the screen in front of him so he could at least follow along.

"This is Governor Dunham," Alla finally appeared on

Aileen's screen, the image a little fuzzy from all the scrambling going on, and the fact that it was a Rio system she was talking on, rather than something Alla would be used to.

"Hello, Governor," Aileen smiled at the image.

"Aileen!" Alla cried out and smiled. "What news from home?"

"Addison and Lazarus took Oton Mari," she explained, starting into details about how she had ended up here. Nothing was going on around her, other than Marie quietly issuing orders and Briston fidgeting.

Just for the hell of it, Aileen reached over and took his closer hand in hers, holding and maybe grounding him a little. She still remembered the first time she had walked into a room full of Humans and had to impress them. Them all being storks hadn't helped, but she hadn't given a shit then, and wasn't about to now.

"So now there may be a battle overhead?" Alla asked as Aileen finished up her news, hoping that she'd pushed the right button and recorded everything. Just so she didn't have to repeat herself fourteen million times after this.

"That's what the Admiral suspects," Aileen replied, not figuring that she was really giving away any military secrets, with as many warships as were maneuvering around.

It was weird, too. Because they could step through space portals instead of using trans-space tunnels, Westphalian ships could sit out there a little ways, and then jump right down on some poor victim. But then, Lazarus had done the same thing. The only real difference had been that he had managed to sneak up on the system whereas Carlos knew they were coming.

Plus, Carlos could hide in the shadow of the station that had since been completed. Big guns protecting everyone.

"Hang on," Aileen said, putting the circuit on mute at

this end so that Alla could see her, but not hear as Aileen turned to Marie Oslor, who had apparently turned into another one of those important people that stories would get written about, like Aileen, but was really just there at the right time.

Lt. Oslor muted her screen and smiled back.

"How much can I tell the folks on the ground?" Aileen asked.

"Not a lot," Marie said, her face pulling sideways in the same manner than Aileen's whiskers would have done, were the situation reversed. "They're civilians, and even the governor doesn't have a security clearance for this sort of thing. Plus, I know from conversations with Eha and the others that most of your kin don't really understand all this military stuff."

"Ain't that the truth," Aileen nodded. "Before I met Lazarus, I had never encountered a warlike species. What you people do to each other still frightens me."

Oslor grimaced and shrugged, and that seemed to sum it all up. Humans were crazy, violent, and held the key to freeing the galaxy in their furless hands.

Aileen turned back to her screen.

"Alla, keep someone close to monitor this channel, and I'll send occasional updates, but mostly by burst text rather than making you a target," Aileen said firmly. "Don't tell everyone else right now, and just keep folks going about their day as much as possible, okay? There's nothing anybody down there can do right now except panic."

Alla nodded and signed off, which was just as well, because a few moments later, someone in the background yelled the word that made all Aileen's fur stand up.

"Contact."

FORTY-SEVEN

CARLOS

CARLOS HAD BEEN GAMING this out for months. Almost from the moment that he'd heard about the first battle over Vilga when *Ajax* chased off a Westphalian fleet. Certainly since he hit that ScoutWall in Innruld Space.

There had been no doubt in his mind that Earth would send another force here at some point. Having Churquen and Yithadreph pilots who could give them the coordinates they needed would be the reason to try again.

And, contrary to all logic, them coming as soon as they could worked in his favor. The Westphalian Admirals must have thought that they could sneak up and catch him off guard.

Yeah, fat chance, seaweasels.

Carlos studied the screen in front of him and took note of what it displayed.

He had *Recife* and a squadron of Light Starcruisers. Everyone's escorts, plus the team *Ajax* had left here originally. Oh, and a forward operating base. With guns. Lots of guns.

Not enough to make him happy and certainly not enough for complacency, but Carlos had everyone moving all the time so nobody could step out of jump in a blind spot. The only wildcard was the colony. He'd dropped a full battalion of marines to the surface with instructions to build up a small search and rescue capability while preparing for combat with orbital forces. Nothing to hurt big ships, but they had a couple of batteries of guns capable of sweeping the skies clear over the colony if some idiot tried to land hostile shuttles.

The invaders could still come in wide, land over the horizon, and drive trucks over, but that was it. No risk that someone would be able to drop in a team and kidnap Alla easily.

"Command," Carlos called, getting everyone's attention. "Order the station to combat operations independent of the squadrons. Let them snipe at anyone who gets close enough for now. What are we facing?"

"Signals just coming in," Oslor called back. "Two Heavies. Two Lights and a GunWall in front of them as escorts. Standing well off and holding position."

Holding position? That made no sense, but maybe they didn't want to immediately attack?

It was a balanced fight, on the surface of things. He had one Heavy and four Lights, so the sides were about evenly matched if you counted the station and the escort squadrons flying around. Still, one hell of a major fleet incursion by Westphalia. Carlos was just sorry he didn't have *Ajax* here right now to kill things for him.

He'd seen the specs Lazarus put together. And everyone had seen video of *Gotland* tumbling ass over teakettle.

"Signal," Oslor sang out. "Beam fire. Stand by."

Carlos turned to watch the woman, and noted the two Yithadreph sitting next to her, apparently holding hands, but he hadn't seen any hint of romance earlier. Maybe just comforting the new kid?

"Admiral, Heavy Starcruiser *Mannheim* just fired a shot across our bow from extreme range," she said with an angry snarl to her voice.

"Across?" he confirmed.

"Affirmative, sir."

So, they wanted to play, did they? So confident that he would just strike his colors and flee?

Let's find out.

Carlos had commanded a Patrol Cruiser for the last five years. Fragile long-sailors, under-gunned against anything they were likely to encounter, but capable of going from here to a farther *there* faster than anything but a Courier.

"All vessels hold fire," he ordered. "Station included. Everyone turn away and prepare to rendezvous here."

He marked a spot on his screen almost next to the station, a few degrees latitude away but not all that much. Hiding beneath the umbrella of the big guns, as it were.

"Jump as you bear," Carlos ordered with a chuckle, hoping that his people would hear it and convey to the folks on comms that the Admiral in charge was amused, not frightened.

Redshift. Around him, blueshifts as other vessels did the same. The formation was a little ragged, but it had been a short hop, and probably nobody had been prepared for something that deep in the tactics manual.

Hopefully, the Earthers were also scratching their heads just as much. If they came to where he was right now, they'd be nearly point-blank to the big guns on the station.

"What's he doing now?"

"Watching, sir," Oslor replied. "Lot of encrypted traffic over there. Probably up seventy-five percent over normal."

Talking. Lots of talking. And maybe head-scratching.

Humans were an aggressive species. The Dunhams and all the other colonists he had encountered all shared that opinion. Violence at the drop of a hat. Gnashiiley weren't so much, but he'd had any suggestion of passivity bounced out of him a long time ago.

Now, he needed to look good. Weren't that many Gnashiiley admirals in the fleet. Didn't want any of them catching any shit from their peers because of him.

"Command, signal *PL-371* and open a channel," Carlos called, letting Marie route everything until Rodriguez appeared in a comm window on his screen.

"Sir?" the man asked.

"Gunter, I have a special prize for you," Carlos laughed. "I want all three of your ships to open fire on *Mannheim*. Simultaneous shots on your command. One from each vessel."

"Across his bow or into his snout, Admiral?" Gunter Rodriguez asked.

"Boop him, Rodriguez," Carlos said, his tone turning cold and hard now. "Goad him like a bull. Can't imagine they're dumb enough to jump into a trap like this, but everyone else will be ready to stomp on *Mannheim* if he does."

"Roger, sir," the Commander of *PL-371* said. "Stand by."

"Command, all vessels," Carlos continued. "When I give the command, any spare guns with arc are to be fired on *Mannheim* until ordered otherwise, regardless of range or better targets. Punish their flag to your own detriment if you have to, but let me know if you start getting overloaded so we can come over and stomp on someone for you."

This time, his crew started to chuckle. They were all Rod da Silva's men and women, except for Marie, Aileen, and the newcomer. Da Silva would have probably sailed right up to *Mannheim* and gotten into a slugging match with them.

They had most likely showed up here today expecting that.

Whoops.

"Two hits, extreme range," Marie called over the comm. "Minimal damage."

About what Carlos had been expecting. Maybe enough oomph to give a Human a reasonable tan at this range, but not enough to spall off chunks of steel and alloys.

Not the point.

"Command, all vessels," Carlos followed up. "Everyone except the station start pouring fire into *Mannheim*'s nose. Stand by for them to either sail down to stop us or to do something stupid like short jump. Station hold fire until ordered."

It didn't help that Carlos had been reading up on the tactics Lazarus had used here. And even interviewed the man afterwards. *The Ajax Retrograde* was just an insane tactical maneuver. Everyone had engines aft to push, even though you rode gravitational waves rather than thrust generated by burning propellant.

There was absolutely no reason not to walk backwards in front of someone, punching him, except that nobody had thought of it until Addison Wolcott had asked. And none of these ships had been designed for something like that. Optimum for them was a broadside that allowed rear guns to rotate perpendicular to the hull.

Y'all come down here and try to cross my 'lee, pickles.

Oldest maneuver in sailing. Your guns turned broadside while he sailed forward, with only half his guns able to fire back. If the enemy was in a column when you formed a Capital-T across their line, all of your ships could pour fire into his sequentially.

In layman's terms, a slaughter.

He laughed out loud as everyone opened up now. Extreme range, even for a Star Lance, but nobody was moving relative, so that made it easier to calculate deflections at this range.

"Enemy squadron in motion," Marie called out. "Inbound, medium speed."

Carlos grinned. Nobody likes just standing there and being slapped, even if kittens might hit harder at this range. But he'd already forced Westphalia into their second mistake. They had given up tactical advantage by deciding to issue a formal duel instead of just charging him. Now, they were going to waddle their silly asses down to wrestle with him in the mud.

He expected that someone was paying attention to the station. They had designed it, after all, and Rio hadn't done much to change it, other than just finish it off and maybe add a few extra guns and docking rings.

Things were about to get silly, even as serious as they were.

FORTY-EIGHT

AILEEN

AILEEN STUDIED the vectors of moment. It helped when she thought of them as one-foot-cubed shipping boxes that she was needing to put in some order. It stopped being chaos at that point and turned into a symphony of organization.

Stupid way to fight, to do anything, but Humans were not the most logical creatures in the galaxy.

"What are they doing?" Briston stage whispered, leaning a little closer than he had been before.

Aileen trapping his hand in her lap didn't help.

"So we've got all these green dots," Aileen said. "We're the star and the station is the big circle. All the red dots are Westphalia. *Mannheim* is their flagship, that big one in the center as they charge us. Lazarus said they tended to sail in waves, so you have all those GunWall ships up front, then the Light Starcruisers behind them. Then the biggest ships at the rear."

"Why do it that way?" he asked.

"All the ships pretty much come into fighting range at the same time," Aileen replied, falling back on her correspondence courses in military maneuver.

Silly damned class, but everyone had to pass it if they wanted to sit a watch on the bridge of a warship. And she had found herself enjoying it.

It helped to think of the little dots as those shipping containers that she was moving around as they got close to Dormell. Even if Humans were going to get killed today.

"And we're not flying in layers like that?" Briston asked, gesturing with his off hand.

Carlos Nguema had his forces in a crescent, tips pointed at the Westphalia formation. That made perfect sense if everyone was going to just hammer on *Mannheim*, but she didn't understand why that would make a big difference. There were two of them, *Mannheim* and *Dresden*, plus several Light Starcruisers.

"Command, all vessels," Carlos filled the big room with his voice. "Begin retrograde motion on this path. Reverse at one quarter power."

Aileen watched the line appear and started to snicker now.

"What?" Briston demanded.

She wondered if anyone else saw it, or if you had to be a Quartermaster in order to get the joke. The Rio force wasn't going straight backwards, but curving slightly, like Addison did when he was trying to hold in the giggles after someone told a particularly bad Dad joke.

"Sucker's bet," Aileen said, tracing the line with her finger. "They follow us here and it curls them right through the best range for the guns on the station to hammer them."

"Why does that matter?" Briston asked, confused now.

"I'm guessing that Carlos comes to a dead stop just as they get close, and then goes right at them," Aileen concluded. "In the confusion, *Mannheim* gets clobbered from two directions."

"You would be right, if it works, Commander," Carlos

called suddenly. "You sure you don't want to make a living at this?"

"Quartermaster Corps, sir," she growled at him with the exact same surliness that Lazarus had gotten more than once. Addison was the only person she knew with less interest in a career in the Rio Alliance Navy.

"So how did you figure it out, then?" Carlos Nguema asked.

"Boxes needing to be packed aboard *Shiva Zephyr Glaive*," she called back, aware that she had an audience now. "My hull was a slice of a ring, so things had to flow in and out in a particular manner in order to get them out with a least-motion-solution at the far end, multiplied by every stop we took on our loop."

"Well, hopefully they didn't promote a competent quartermaster to command and give him a fleet, Enjehn," Carlos laughed. "I'd like this to be a surprise."

Others chuckled, so Aileen presumed that the Gnashiiley had been infected with alien thought processes. Churquen or something. She refused to accept any responsibilities for this.

Humans were going to die today. Aileen Enjehn didn't need that on her conscience.

FORTY-NINE

CARLOS

CARLOS WATCHED HIS SCREENS. His forces had been giving ground slowly, relative to the closing force. The station had been allowed a few pot shots with Star Spears only as the Westphalia fleet curled around the outer edge of their guns, but nothing heavier. *Dresden* had fired a few shots in return, but then largely ignored the station.

With any luck, the Westphalian admiral in command would presume that the station was having problems, or didn't have big guns in spite of the design. Or maybe just didn't want to be destroyed in battle. His ships were taking a beating, even backing away and maneuvering, but the formation was designed for this, if not exactly optimized. Full Westphalian GunWall up front, all twenty-one vessels, with the four Starcruisers flying behind them, two Lights on the wings and the Heavies in the center.

His force was clustered differently, with escort squadrons and triads closer and his Light Starcruisers forming a V with the tips forward, even as he withdrew. A smart admiral would have marshaled his forces in a matching line, trusting that his two Lights would make up for lacking a second Heavy.

Hey, you. I'm a buffoon doing dumb things. You should charge me and completely disrupt my formation.

Carlos smiled, checking the clock on his screen and wondering if there was any way to telepathically goad a Human admiral into action.

"Signals," Marie Oslor called. "Enemy force accelerating. Maintaining vector but significant blueshift detected."

"About bloody time, you morons!" Carlos yelled at nobody in particular. Except maybe an enemy commander too far away to hear him. "Command, all vessels cease retrograde, come to rest, and **charge** the Westphalian fleet. Pass below his plane of travel and rendezvous here. Station, cut loose with everything you have immediately and continue. Everyone maintain prior Target Priority: *Mannheim*, *Dresden*, CommandWall vessel, Light Starcruisers. Let's go kill things."

There was a ragged cheer as a purple dot appeared on everyone's screen. The ship's inertial dampers prevented him from feeling the hard pulse of deceleration, but Carlos still felt it in his mind.

He'd been giving ground for nearly two hours. *Rope-a-dope*, the ancients had once called it, but now he was in the late rounds and needed to come out punching.

"Command, contact *Recife*," Carlos followed up. "I'd like you to boop him pretty hard on the nose right now."

"Significant boopage imminent, Admiral," Paulo Quispe called back with a laugh in his voice that was echoed in the backgrounds of both rooms.

Morale, the ancient Marshal had said, was three to one to the *Material*. The Rio fleet should be brimming over with it, right about now.

"Signals, enemy communication traffic has just tripled," Marie called out. "Still unable to crack their crypto, but I'm smelling a little panic, sir."

Carlos nodded at Marie. Once Aileen had pointed it out, he'd watched Marie ask her a few questions, so that corner of the room knew what to look for.

The next two minutes were going to utterly suck, as Westphalia let loose with everything they had, but *Mannheim* and *Dresden* had both already been booped a few times with lucky shots that had scoured their bow shielding like sandpaper.

At the same time, his force knew it was coming, and would be maneuvering madly shortly, so those incoming shots would be a little more wild.

And then the station let loose with a full broadside of Star Lances. Five of the six could arc right here, which was why Carlos had backed *Mannheim* into this particular corner. And booped his snoot a few times, to the degree that he had forgotten to reinforce the shields on that side.

Whoever was in command of the guns over there even sequenced his fire rather than letting loose all at once. Shot number three kissed bare metal after most of it was splashed by the shielding on this face. Four hit like a hammer. Five went in like a knife.

Maybe Vilga's Stand would develop a reputation as the place where Westphalian Heavy Starcruisers went to get crippled, because all of a sudden *Mannheim* was tumbling sideways and spinning on two axes of motion. The tumble wouldn't save them, either, because now every Rio ship in range was splitting his fire between the closest enemy vessel overhead, and *Mannheim*. Shields kept rotating, and gunners were timing shots to hit bare metal if they could.

Fighting a space battle had frequently been described as stabbing someone to death with ice picks. You damaged his shields, and then poked him until maybe he bled to death, but more likely he would run away as fast as he could.

Mannheim couldn't run.

Instead, they suddenly went dark. Carlos had never seen something like that happen, even in his studies. Someone must have gotten the spinal mains, or maybe jarred all the generators off-line. She stopped firing, stopped maneuvering, maybe stopped living.

"Signals, I have a flag transfer from *Mannheim* to *Dresden*," Marie called. "Repeat *Dresden* now in command of enemy squadron."

"All guns, all ships, change targeting," Carlos called. "Kill *Dresden* next."

FIFTY

AILEEN

AILEEN FELT her stomach want to turn over. This was what it meant to be Human. That moment when Carlos the Gnashiiley killed one ship [**_KILLED IT!_**] and nonchalantly moved on to kill the next one.

Around her, *Recife* shuddered as guns on all sides continued to batter it but they had indeed caught the Westphalia force off guard by suddenly rushing past them. Accuracy had fallen drastically for the enemy vessels.

Rio sailors were killing people all around her.

And you people want me to stay around for that?

But she didn't voice those words. At the end of the day, there was no difference between what Carlos the Gnashiiley was doing and what Aileen the Yithadreph had done at places like Aceanx or Zhoonarrim. Aileen wasn't about to suggest that the drugs she had carried, the lives she had destroyed with them, made her any better.

Just as the Innruld would not give way without violence, so would Westphalia plant itself across the middle of the road to stop all progress for anyone who wasn't *Human.*

She felt Briston's hand transmit his own shudders, so she turned to him.

"This is what liberation looks like, Briston Moora," she said in a quiet, firm voice. "The Species Underground has maybe not made it that stark, but this is exactly what Lazarus will be doing over in Innruld Space. Except that in his case, they won't even have as much chance to resist."

"No?" Briston's ears and whiskers were all the way flat back.

"About as much chance as a Galumph has, Briston," she said. "I was with Lazarus when Westphalia tried this last time. It was just as ugly."

"Is this a mistake?" he asked.

"Do you want to be free, kid?" Aileen snapped, maybe a little louder than she thought, because Marie looked this way, as did Carlos Nguema. Aileen stabbed at her screen with a furry finger. "That's what freedom looks like. And what it costs. There are going to be a lot of dead people afterwards. If that's too much for you, then you need to either take up farming on the planet below, or head back to Oton Mari and hide in your machine bays."

He straightened up now. Focused on her, pulling everything forward with a hard flinch.

"They sent me because I was willing to kill people, Enjehn," he said with a pretty good growl. "Even complete strangers. I want to be free, whatever the cost."

She nodded, finding that fire in him finally. Aileen had suspected it, but he'd been on his best behavior up until now, maybe a little intimidated by everything, but this battle had stripped it all bare now, like a bad case of mange.

Around them, the hull rocked again as somebody booped *Recife* pretty hard, but then everything fell to silence.

No, scratch that. Cheers.

Aileen looked around in confusion.

Marie smiled at her and tapped a spot on the screen.

"Where's they go?" Aileen asked dumbly.

"Fled," Marie said before raising her voice to fill the entire room. "Signals. Enemy fleet has withdrawn. *Mannheim* is striking her colors and requesting rescue."

More cheers.

They'd won?

FIFTY-ONE

ADDISON STUDIED the image of Oton Mari station on the new screens that had been installed. After the battle, they had been forced to strip the old bridge of the captured Security Pyramid to the bulkheads to get to all the damage. Every console had been open to space, after being flash-fried by the shot from Cormac that had disabled the vessel.

Dead as a galumph for lunch.

As a result, Addison had supervised the repair crews and rebuilt it exactly the way he wanted. If Addison couldn't have *Shiva Zephyr Glaive*, he could at least make it look as close to the same as possible. That included a cone chair with a slight wobble to the left, a result of too many years of a Churquen Director with a particular twitch when he sat.

Cormac was here, in the same location, relative. There was a new space for a Fusilier to command the enormous overkill of guns, although there were too many for him to fire them himself. Just as well Wybert wasn't here. That part of the design was from *Ajax*.

Next to the Fusilier was the pilot. Again, Kuei was better off flying *Ajax*, so he had Artin Sonez, a Kr'mari male who was young, hungry, and had a deep anger at the Innruld. Worse, the Fusilier who would sit next to him was an old Churquen matron named Lamuen Harden who tended to growl at him whenever the Innruld were mentioned.

At least he would not have to worry about anyone wanting to run away from battle. The big fear he had, looking at the backs of everyone's heads, was that Artin might decide to ram another Pyramid if he thought it was getting away from him. Cormac had added an override at Addison's request, so either of them could take over flying the vessel if they had to.

But everything was repaired now. Working as intended, upgunned and upshielded. They were even flying patrols to get everyone used to this.

"Addison, I believe the Innruld Response has arrived," Cormac suddenly spoke up, his voice falling perfectly flat, like it did when he was overly emotional.

The screen in front of him lit up with the most terrifying image Addison had ever imagined. Five Innruld Security Pyramids *[**FIVE!**]* flying towards him, point first so that all the guns on the top could see him.

"Invader, you will surrender immediately or we will destroy you," a hard Innruld voice came over the comm.

Addison took a deep breath and held it for a second.

"First, make sure that *Ajax* is scanning them," he ordered Cormac, trusting the NavCrawler to handle that task dispassionately. "Second, we have better range. Lamuen, open fire as soon as you can. Artin, back us away from them and keep them in front of us as much as possible. The station can take care of itself for now."

Both growled more than replied, but he took that as a good sign.

Five of them? That was insane!

Addison had a vision of two entire sectors of Innruld

Space stripped of command vessels. If only he knew which two and could send a couple of Rio destroyers over. No Security Barc could withstand a destroyer, even for a minute. The piracy potential would be enormous.

Or maybe they could just start killing Barcs as fast as they could chase them down.

Lamuen's guns cut loose. Most of the turrets were still no better than a Rio Star Spear, but she had six Star Lances mounted. Those ranged from here.

Addison wasn't sure they would be enough, but he was damned sure going to try.

FIFTY-TWO

LAZARUS

LAZARUS WAS out of his office and into his command chair as soon as the alarms sounded. That allowed him the awesome view of Kuei Akeley arriving just after he did.

Everyone always noticed the bottom-heavy tripod of a Vaadwig, that creature that looked like nothing so much as a Terran kangaroo. They would see how she had to waddle awkwardly on two big feet and a tail to move around, and forget that the species was originally made for the open savanna.

Kuei came through the hatch with a quick shuffle, and then hoisted her tail and shot up and forward in a grand bound. She touched down once, coiled like a spring, and launched herself again, landing perfectly next to the junior lieutenant she was replacing.

The Human woman's mouth fell completely open. Lazarus smiled.

Wybert had already been on duty as Fusilier today, so he was there. Lazarus watched him drum his feet once, right rear to right front, then left front to left rear, a muffled sound because Kuei had added a pad to the deck all the way around.

"Bring the ship to combat readiness," Lazarus ordered in a big voice.

He mashed his hand down on the button that caused all the sirens to wind up and the lights to shift to red.

"Mother of God," he gasped when the sensors finally identified the mess.

Addison had renamed his vessel *Vigilant*, rather than *Venger* or something equally hostile. Right now, all of his Star Lances were hammering away at the two closest Security Pyramids, bashing away at the shields harder than any Innruld-built hull had a right to.

But those were Rio guns. And the commander over there was a Rio Captain, much as Addison disliked admitting it.

Admiral da Silva came through the hatch at a hard jog now, throwing himself into a nearby station and powering things on. They had a flag bridge aft where Rod could have worked, but didn't really have a crew to command, and this squadron wasn't going to act like one, either.

"Status?" Rod asked.

"Five Innruld Pyramids, Rod," Lazarus said. "Just dropped out of trans-space and ordered everyone to surrender or be destroyed. Addison is withdrawing in front of them and engaging at max range as they pursue."

"I see," Rod said phlegmatically. "Far be it for me to issue you maneuver orders, Captain, but I would greatly appreciate us riding to Addison's rescue right now. I only have one Churquen Captain, so I need to keep him alive."

"Cross their T?" Lazarus looked over and smiled.

"Yes," Rod smiled back. "That would do nicely, Lazarus."

"Pilot," Lazarus turned to Kuei now. "Plot their vector and pick a spot where we will be at optimum range for Kirov, when we are ninety degrees or so off their flight path.

Fusilier, hit them with everything except Kirov until we get to that position, then go to rapid fire, shutting everything down but the Kirov as you do to conserve power and minimize the recharge cycle."

Kuei just looked over a shoulder at him and nodded. She didn't like combat, but would do it as professionally as anyone he'd ever flown with. And more artistically.

Wybert flexed his entire body from mandibles to poop chute, clacking his spinnerets once as he did. That was Ilount excitement.

Grace was suddenly seated at a station next to Rod, though Lazarus had never seen her enter. But you didn't. One moment, nothing, the next moment a beautiful woman materialized in front of you and changed your entire day. She'd really had nothing important to do since they captured *Vigilant*, so she had been training members of the Species Underground in a variety of close combat techniques that were at once utterly foreign to those folks, and naturally suited to the various body shapes and strengths.

She smiled at him now, and it was like the sun had come out on a cloudy day.

"All hands," he called into the ship-wide intercom. "Stand by for combat. The Innruld have brought two entire sector fleets to contest our control of Oton Mari. Five enemy Pyramids. Gunners, I'm sorry to announce that they didn't bring anything little for you to shoot at, so it will be an all-big-guns kind of day, at least until they break and we start chasing."

Rod chuckled. Around the ship, Lazarus imagined that a number of other folks did as well.

"Bridge, this is Engineering," H'Brige Slani came through now. "Wybert has told us what he planned. Should we just shut down power and heat to sections of the vessel not currently occupied?"

Lazarus considered it. Wouldn't be much of a difference, but it might still be one extra shot, once the Innruld panicked and started to run. They took a while to get into trans-space, just because they were so huge.

"Go ahead, H'Brige," Lazarus said. "This battle will probably be short and brutal when it hits, so I'll need everything. Your damage control teams can fix things up later."

"Roger that, sir," she said and cut the line.

Lazarus watched the vector plots come up. He had three Star Lances, one on each of his pylons. Addison had six, like a Heavy Starcruiser, but they were jury-rigged, engineers having to literally cut out a section of hull to replace a smaller gun and run a bunch of new wires and cooling systems.

Fragile, maybe, but they were firing slowly now, and one of the Pyramids was already hurt.

That still left four undamaged and coming for his friend.

"It's time," Lazarus said simply, pausing just enough for dramatic tension.

Kuei and Wybert both glanced back inward at him.

"Charge."

FIFTY-THREE

ADDISON

ADDISON HAD HAD nightmares about a battle like this. Him about to be overwhelmed by the entire might of the Innruld and all their thugs and lackeys, when there was nothing he could do about it. Artin was slipping backwards and sideways to get away, but a Pyramid was never designed to maneuver like that. They backed up when they needed to maneuver in orbit, not in combat.

The five in front of them were coming on relentlessly, one in the center and the others on the corners of a box with Addison on the center of the opposite face.

"*Addison, I have identified the enemy flagship,*" Cormac announced suddenly with a chuckle utterly at odds with an electronic life form. "*They are using a standard encryption key on their communications. One I can break.*"

"Tell *Ajax,*" Addison said. "Lamuen, stay with your current target until you hurt him. The worst thing we could do is spread our fire out and injure all of them a little. We need to kill one."

"That lets the others hurt us," she replied.

"Only briefly, Fusilier," Addison replied.

Around them, the hull rocked once. Not much and not bad. Innruld heavy powerbolts were finally ranging well enough to still pack a punch when they hit. Like a Star Spear, but less effective.

But they would be able to pound him mercilessly once all of them could reach.

Addison watched the screens. He'd been through enough self-training for a Rio combat officer to recognize what *Ajax* was doing. He would have liked Kuei to get here sooner, but he supposed that the Pyramids needed to be lured into position.

More bangs on the hull now as he listened.

"How are our shields holding?" he asked.

"*Seventy percent on facing and falling,*" Cormac replied. "*We will be critical in six minutes.*"

I hope you're listening, Lazarus. In six minutes I'll be in serious trouble.

FIFTY-FOUR

LAZARUS

"CONFIRMED?" Lazarus asked, just as a matter of habit.

"It's Cormac," Kuei replied with a hint of disappointment at him.

"Right, sorry," Lazarus said. "Training. Fusilier, change your targeting priority. I want that ship killed hard first. Star Lances, have the Fusilier identify a target for you and be prepared to open up on them from extremely close range when we all blow by each other at high speed."

His board blinked green as all the Gun Captains acknowledged.

Vigilant was giving better than it got, but there were still five of them, four in good shape and one limping from the thrashing Addison's team had given it.

"Captain, we are in range to execute a crossing," Wybert announced in that high, bird-like tone of his.

"Fusilier, engage as you bear," Lazarus said.

And that was that.

He had just turned Wybert of Capantzina loose to kill whoever and however he felt like it, in the most powerful, dangerous warship in the galaxy.

Lazarus flashed back to a conversation with Aileen and Khyaa'sha, early in his stay with the gang on *Shiva Zephyr Glaive*, when he had described Wybert as a little soft in the head.

After today, the queens would be lining up to mate with him. With Wybert.

Weird.

"Firing," Wybert announced unnecessarily.

Kirov's Lance fluoresced the solar wind between here and there a soft blue for a long eyeblink.

They had an optical telescope centered on each target, along with a variety of sensors and scanners. Lazarus watched the first shot slice the enemy flagship into two pieces like a carving knife preparing a turkey for Christmas dinner.

Wybert had adjusted the targeting of the beam even in the flash it fired. The top several decks were suddenly disconnected from the vessel, with a huge flare of plasma driving the two pieces in different directions as the cloud expanded.

Huh. Wybert had just decapitated the flagship. That was a novel approach. And one of the reasons Rio warships put the command spaces as close to the central spine of the ship as possible.

"Firing," Wybert repeated.

A second Pyramid staggered, the shot entering through the top where they kept their bridge and exiting close to a base corner, like a lava tube carved through a mountain.

"Enemy vessels are now maneuvering to escape my wrath," Wybert continued in a flat, observational voice. "Suckers."

Lazarus just shook his head and imagined Ilount queens flying personally to Rio Space to find the legendary killer Wybert of Capantzina. The stud Liberator. That was going to be interesting.

"What the hell is Addison doing?" Kuei spoke up.

"Talk to me," Lazarus called.

"*Vigilant* just stopped dead, using max acceleration to kill all their forward momentum when nobody was looking," Kuei said. "The outer four are about to blow right by him, and the dead one might still clip him in passing."

"Assume he has a plan," Lazarus replied. "Maintain our current operations until he says something."

Vigilant was going to be hurt, except that the three living ones, two undamaged and one mauled, were probably about to start running like hell.

"Firing," Wybert called to the quiet bridge.

FIFTY-FIVE

ADDISON

ADDISON TURNED TO STUDY CORMAC.

"You're sure?" he asked.

"*Current flight vectors indicate that the rear section of that vessel will miss us by at least two hundred feet, Addison,*" Cormac replied.

"Artin, I'd prefer three hundred feet, but go ahead and bring us to rest, relative to the planet right now," Addison said. "As long as they don't hit us. Lamuen, fire everything you have. And keep firing it. They are about to panic and try running, but we've trapped them in the middle of a killing zone and we need to hold them for *Ajax*. Everything can be repaired after *Ajax* chases them off, and if they get too close to the station hunting us later, there's another surprise waiting."

"Yes, sir," Lamuen said in a shaky voice.

Artin just waved a hand in…something. Maybe acknowledgment. Or killing fury. The Kr'mari looked like he wanted to start dancing, from his body language.

Around them, the lights flickered as the draw on the generators swelled. For nearly two seconds, the room went almost pitch black, but then everything returned to normal, just about when the emergency lights would have come on.

Vigilant might have to be scrapped after this, but Lamuen and her gun teams weren't taking a lot of return fire as they lashed out. Everyone else was just trying to escape the wolf that had appeared in their midst, too busy trying to save themselves to remember to shoot at their original victim.

Addison wondered if his people were just going to melt everything, but even if everyone on this ship died, they'd already struck a terrible blow against Innruld control.

Something popped and the room went dark, but Addison smiled.

Liberation was at hand.

FIFTY-SIX

GRACE

GRACE WATCHED the man in his native element. This was the Lazarus she had fallen in love with. Hard, pure, tough, but still brilliant and empathic when he needed to be. Lazarus was in perfect synch with Kuei Akeley and Wybert of Capantzina, much like a professional team of dancers.

Around them, *Ajax* meted out punishment on the Innruld ships like a farmer selecting chickens for dinner. Those Pyramids had about as much chance today.

She became aware of Rio Alliance Admiral Roderick da Silva studying her, so Grace glanced over at the man.

"Do me a favor?" he whispered.

Grace was intrigued. Da Silva wasn't someone she had interacted with directly all that much. Mostly, the man worked with Lazarus and Addison when he needed to do things. As a civilian, and not even a Rio citizen, Grace would have thought she was beneath his notice.

"Perhaps," Grace offered, mostly to see what the man might desire from a woman like her.

"When you all are living in the former Innruld Space full time, remind Lazarus to come back to Brasilia occasionally?"

da Silva asked. "He won't remember, and won't want to come, but all of this is a direct result of his excellence."

"What makes you think that, Admiral?" she countered.

"We have not treated *Pancho* Oliveira all that well, Grace," da Silva grimaced. "He did the impossible, more than once, and was insulted, demeaned, and questioned at every step. I was about the only person willing to stand up for him, which is why Pedro Santos sent me with *Dutra*. Lazarus will remember that when he's destroyed the Innruld, and I suspect he would rather spend the rest of his life with you, most likely here, rather than return to Rio space."

Grace managed to not show the shock she felt. Her face was perfectly composed. Even a chiseled eyebrow managed the perfect amount of curiosity. She and Lazarus had had a similar conversation, snuggled in their cabin, not two days ago.

"The Rio Alliance will expand, Grace," the Admiral said. "Has, if anyone at or around Vilga has the brains God gave a goose. Eha and Alla Dunham. All the colonists. It is only a matter of time."

"What about Westphalia?" she asked.

"That's why I want you to remind him," da Silva said. "We still need to finish the Earthers off."

FIFTY-SEVEN

LAZARUS

LAZARUS REVIEWED THE WRECKAGE. There was a considerable amount of it scattered around and only slowly being captured by the gravity of the planet beneath them.

Vigilant had survived. It was about in as bad a shape as it had been right after Cormac blew the hell out of it at point blank with a Star Spear against no shields.

Two of the Pyramids had surrendered with damage minimal enough that truly committed Directors could have justified fighting on or maybe managing to flee far enough to try to get to trans-space.

Three of them were scrap metal. One had literally exploded, a chain reaction hitting something like a fuel cell and overloading it, blowing a second, a third, et cetera until what was left looked like an orange peel that had been taken off in two pieces.

He opened a channel to *Vigilant*. Cormac located Addison and put him on the screen in what looked like a private office. His old friend and former director looked worn out.

"You have a crew that can handle the repairs, Addison,"

Lazarus reminded him. "A Captain doesn't need to do more than tour some of the damaged areas and then let his crew take care of it."

Addison sighed.

"This was never my idea, Lazarus," he explained. "It is, to quote you, merely necessary. This crew is not a team of Rio sailors intent on saving the galaxy, like yours. They need to see me. To hear me. To know that we have liberated them from the Innruld, and they will, in turn, go on to liberate other systems until the masters of the galaxy are gone."

"How much force did they lose here?" Lazarus asked. "What do six Security Pyramids amount to, as a fraction of the overall whole?"

"Perhaps five percent," Addison admitted, still weary from his voice. "Enough that whole sectors have nothing but much smaller Security Barcs protecting them and policing the population right now. But the job is not done."

"Correct," Lazarus agreed. "They have been rocked back on their heels hard. Control will start to slip. I intend to make some quick voyages to a few places, expressly for the purpose of blowing up more such Pyramids. Maybe I will even strike at Innruld itself, just to set terror loose in their hearts. I need you to do one thing for me."

"What's that?" Addison asked, eyes narrowing.

"You will be the military commander of Oton Mari for a month or so while I'm gone," Lazarus explained. "But I need you to train folks to replace you."

"Replace me?" Addison blinked, surprised.

"When I get back, you and I are going to Vilga, my friend," Lazarus said. "We're going to see your mate and your family."

"Oh," Addison said. "Right. Then what?"

"Then you and I are going to go destroy Westphalia."

Addison fell silent, like he could not imagine such a task.

But a week ago, defeating five Security Pyramids was an impossible task. Until it had been done.

"Captains, I have an alert," Kuei's voice broke in. "Blueshift detected, but out a bit. There is a vessel at those coordinates, and I am getting hailed."

"Addison, get yourself ready to command, just in case this is trouble, but I double Westphalia would have come here," Lazarus said. "Kuei, wake the admiral."

"Who would it be then?" Addison asked.

"The signal reads *Celestial Sovereign*," Kuei said. "Does that mean anything?"

Lazarus laughed.

"That is Eduardo Martìnez's yacht," he said. "Someone has finally sailed here from Yisan. Have them bounce in and set coordinates for a rendezvous. Addison, you and Cormac come over here for a meeting."

"Trouble?" Addison asked.

"Not for us."

FIFTY-EIGHT

OLUCHI

OLUCHI STOOD on the bridge of Eduardo's boat and watched over Antonia's shoulder.

And remembered to close his mouth at least twice. Anya had an arm around his waist and he could feel her surprise as well.

"What the hell are those things?" he asked.

"From the shape of the two still intact I would presume those are the things called Security Pyramids," Antonia replied with a laconic voice. "One of them identifies as *Vigilant* on a standard Rio channel. Three of them are dead. Is *Ajax* that lethal?"

"Yes," both he and Anya managed to speak at the same moment.

He hugged her close and contemplated.

Up until now, it had been a theoretical thing, Rio's technical edge on the Innruld. He had been aboard one of those primitive vessels, but Oluchi wasn't an engineer.

Here, however, orbital space above Oton Mari was a graveyard, filling with the fading dreams of *Innruld Galactic Supremacy*.

"*Ajax* is hailing," Antonia said. "Rendezvous and coordinates."

"Good, you will come with us, Antonia," Oluchi decided.

"I will?" She looked up, surprised.

"I'm going to need you," he said.

AJAX HAD NOT CHANGED. Aileen wasn't here, having apparently missed him flying the other direction, but the other key players in Innruld Space were present, once they got through the ceremonial parts.

Lazarus, Addison, and Admiral da Silva sat around a round table, interspersed with him, Anya, and Antonia. Grace and Cormac felt more like observers than anything.

Oluchi glared at Admiral da Silva.

"I'm carrying messages and packages from Vilga," he began sternly, staring directly at the admiral, "but *Celestial Sovereign* is a civilian vessel and you will not impress it into duty as a Rio Auxiliary warship."

"Is it even armed?" da Silva asked dismissively, but Lazarus interrupted a response by laughing.

"Better than anything less than a Pyramid, Rod," he said. "Consider it a light escort for comparison."

"Oh?"

"And not a Rio-flagged vessel," Oluchi cut him off before the man got started on whatever he was thinking.

"So what is your goal here, Oluchi?" Lazarus asked.

"Line of communication from Admiral Nguema, plus news from home," he smiled evilly at them.

"Admiral?" da Silva sat up straighter.

"Santos promoted him, and put him aboard *Recife*," Oluchi smiled. "That squadron and some others went to

Vilga to reinforce the place. I was able to convince Antonia to let me borrow Eduardo's yacht to come here, so I have message packs, news. Oh, and pictures."

That last when Anya reached over and poked him hard in the ribs.

Anya produced a stack of images printed on paper and slid them across the table to Addison as Oluchi continued his silent staring contest with da Silva.

"You have a daughter, Addison," Anya said. "Her name is Adriana and she was the first child ever born on Vilga. And the first Churquen born in the Rio Alliance."

Oluchi allowed da Silva to get distracted, but he understood that the battle was recessed, not over. Still, the pictures changed things some. Lightened the mood.

"Okay, so why are you really here?" Lazarus finally asked, after everyone had congratulated Addison and gotten things relaxed.

"Trade," Oluchi said. "I'm an Ambassador-At-Large for Yisan, as well as Vilga, so it is in my best interests to see about building networks through Akeley's Passage and other things. Plus, nobody knew what was going on here since *Dutra* left."

Oluchi listened as the three men took turns filling in the details of Oton Mari and all that happened. Of what was coming.

In turn, he told them about Brasilia, and his estimation that there had probably been another battle over Vilga by now, but nobody would know that outcome for a while.

Lazarus had fallen silent, like that man got when he was being sneaky.

"You want more *Letters of Marque and Reprisal?*" he asked, looking at Oluchi and Antonia. "Issued by the Species Underground this time instead of just the Rio Alliance?"

"Why?" Antonia asked bluntly.

"The Security Barcs you encounter out here will not be in your class for firepower, shielding, or speed," Lazarus said. "They represent no threat to *Celestial Sovereign*, as long as you stay away from Pyramids."

"What will you be doing?" Oluchi asked.

"*Ajax* and I will be out hunting, but we're going after big ships," Lazarus replied. "Killing Pyramids until there are no more, and the Innruld lose the sword that they have been holding over everyone else for so long."

"Is there anything worth stealing?" Oluchi asked.

"Ships," the man smiled at him now. "We can't build modern ships out here that fast, but if we capture them from the Innruld, especially Barcs, the Species Underground will be able to start manning them quickly enough. Doubly so when word gets out. At some point, it starts a chain reaction."

"You think Eduardo will be happy with me as a pirate, Captain?" Antonia asked.

"Maybe," Lazarus said. "Maybe not. But this will put you in the middle of things here. And Oluchi, I have a job for you, if you are interested."

"What's that?" he asked, cards close to the vest like he was back at Eduardo's table with high stakes on the felt.

Instead of answering, Lazarus turned to the Admiral and studied him for a moment.

"At some level, Innruld control is broken, Rod," Lazarus said. "At least for now. If we range out like Vikings for a month, it will get worse. *Ajax* needs a time in drydock for refurb as well as full resupply. I can only get that at Brasilia. Do you want to come with me there, or remain here?"

"Aren't I supposed to be in charge, Lazarus?" da Silva asked, but everyone around the table was smiling, including the admiral.

"I seem to remember that your orders were to open

negotiations with the Innruld," Lazarus said. "Presumably, to get shot at and then shoot back, when they proved hostile. We don't own Innruld Space right now, but we might in another year or three. Should you be here, supervising the War of Liberation?"

"You're going to Brasilia?" the man asked.

"Assuming Eha and Adriana are there and not Vilga, yes, Rod," Lazarus answered. "I plan to haul back messages from you and communications from this front."

"And Addison?" he asked, nodding to the man still fawning over pictures of his love and his daughter and largely ignoring the room except to perk up now when his name was spoken.

"I'd like to take him with me, as well as his old crew," Lazarus said.

"Where's that leave me?" da Silva asked.

"With an Ambassador to Yisan, Vilga, and possibly the Rio Alliance, assuming everyone negotiated in good faith," Lazarus replied in a most evil voice, one finger coming up to point this way. "Oluchi Pryce."

In spite of himself, Oluchi flinched. It didn't help when Anya snorted under her breath.

"Me?" Oluchi demanded quietly.

Lazarus turned those heavy eyes this way like weapon turrets tracking.

"Do you know anyone closer to the center of negotiations between the Species Underground and the Rio Alliance government, Pryce?" he asked in a hard, quiet voice. "Yisan presumably allies with Rio, so that puts you at the center of everything. I don't want it. Addison doesn't want it. Rod here is a career military man, so at worst he needs you to advise on damned near everything. And Eha trusts you."

Oluchi would not blush, damn it. Even when he did, and the others laughed, which made it worse.

He drew a hot breath to argue with the man, and Anya poked him again. He turned and she smiled.

"Shut up and accept it, Pryce," she grinned. "Or I'll make you go back to Leena."

He couldn't help the shudder that ran through his frame. Obviously, he'd been away from the poker table for too long, that his emotions were this close to the surface.

The others laughed again.

"I seem to be outvoted, Lazarus," Oluchi said. "I appear to be your civilian ambassador, along with the Admiral in a military role. What is it you need me to do at this end, while you are working from Yisan, Vilga, and Brasilia?"

He watched Lazarus of Bethany take a deep breath that seemed to echo down all of history.

"Alliance, Pryce," he said simply.

"Alliance?"

"The Species Underground, the Merchants of Yisan, and the entirety of Rio, bound together and going after Westphalia. I want to break those bastards, once and for all."

Oluchi felt the magnetic power in the man as he spoke. The raw charisma. The brains. The drive that had taken him from the slums to the pinnacle.

Oluchi held out his hand and Lazarus took it.

"I'll do my damnedest," Oluchi promised.

READ MORE

Be sure to read all the books in the Lazarus Alliance series!

Escape
Return
Rebellion
Revolution
Liberation
Retribution
Alliance

Available at your favorite retailers!

ABOUT THE AUTHOR

Blaze Ward writes science fiction in the Alexandria Station universe (Jessica Keller, The Science Officer, The Story Road, etc.) as well as several other science fiction universes, such as Star Dragon, the Dominion, and more. He also writes odd bits of high fantasy with swords and orcs. In addition, he is the Editor and Publisher of *Boundary Shock Quarterly Magazine*. You can find out more at his website www.blazeward.com, as well as Facebook, Goodreads, and other places.

Blaze's works are available as ebooks, paper, and audio, and can be found at a variety of online vendors. His newsletter comes out regularly, and you can also follow his blog on his website. He really enjoys interacting with fans, and looks forward to any and all questions—even ones about his books!

Never miss a release!
If you'd like to be notified of new releases, sign up for my newsletter.

http://www.blazeward.com/newsletter/

Buy More!
Did you know that you can buy directly from my website?

https://www.blazeward.com/shop/

ABOUT KNOTTED ROAD PRESS

Knotted Road Press fiction specializes in dynamic writing set in mysterious, exotic locations.

Knotted Road Press non–fiction publishes autobiographies, business books, cookbooks, and how–to books with unique voices.

Knotted Road Press creates DRM–free ebooks as well as high–quality print books for readers around the world.

With authors in a variety of genres including literary, poetry, mystery, fantasy, and science fiction, Knotted Road Press has something for everyone.

Knotted Road Press
www.KnottedRoadPress.com

www.ingramcontent.com/pod-product-compliance
Lightning Source LLC
Chambersburg PA
CBHW060247100726
47907CB00003B/795